CLAIRE McNAB

DEATH CLUB

BELLA
BOOKS
2017

Bella Books, Inc.
P.O. Box 10543
Tallahassee, FL 32302

First Published by Naiad Press 2001
First Bella Books Edition 2017

Printed in the United States of America on acid-free paper

Editor: Lila Empson
Cover Designer: Sandy Knowles

ISBN 13: 978-1-931513-46-3

Other Bella Books by Claire McNab

Under the Southern Cross
Silent Heart
Writing My Love

Carol Ashton Series:
Lessons in Murder
Fatal Reunion
Death Down Under
Cop Out
Dead Certain
Body Guard
Double Bluff
Inner Circle
Chain Letter
Past Due
Set Up
Under Suspicion
Death Club
Accidental Murder
Blood Link
Fall Guy

Denise Cleever Series:
Murder Undercover
Death Understood
Out of Sight
Recognition Factor
Death by Death
Murder at Random

Kylie Kendall Series:
The Wombat Strategy
The Kookaburra Gambit
The Quokka Question
The Dingo Dilemma
The Platypus Ploy

For Sheila and Sophie

Acknowledgments

My deepest appreciation goes to my patient, good-humored, and superlative editor, Lila Empson, and also to my typesetter—a wonderful woman in every way. Thanks also to Judy Eda for her skills in proofreading.

About the Author

Claire McNab is the author of thirteen Detective Inspector Carol Ashton mysteries: *Lessons in Murder, Fatal Reunion, Death Down Under, Cop Out, Dead Certain, Body Guard, Double Bluff, Inner Circle, Chain Letter, Past Due, Set Up, Under Suspicion,* and *Death Club.* She has written two romances, *Under the Southern Cross* and *Silent Heart,* and has co-authored a self-help book, *The Loving Lesbian,* with Sharon Gedan. She is the author of two Denise Cleever thrillers, *Murder Undercover* and *Death Understood.* Her third Denise Cleever thriller, *Out of Sight,* will be published in fall of 2001.

In her native Australia Claire is known for her crime fiction, plays, children's novels, and self-help books.

Now permanently residing in Los Angeles, she teaches fiction writing in the UCLA Extension Writers' Program. She makes it a point to return to Australia once a year to refresh her Aussie accent.

PROLOGUE

The rim of the sun broke the horizon, and instantly a dazzling yellow-gold stream ran across the ocean's surface to the land.

"Pull up here."

The golf cart slowed at the top of the cliff where the treacherous fourth hole of the Whitlew Country Club was situated. Countless balls had missed the green and plummeted down the sheer sandstone to splash into the heaving surf below.

Squinting, Joe Gallagher put up his hand to shade his eyes. "Ah, Jesus," he said. "Some bastard's put something in the sand trap."

There was a note of possessive anger in his voice. He was responsible for every tee, every fairway, every green, and in preparation for the Whitlew Challenge he had groomed the course to perfection. It was the second day of the tournament, and, as was his custom, he was doing a dawn check of every hole before his crew of workers was out on the course.

His assistant stretched his neck to peer in the direction of the bunker. "How could anyone get in?" he asked. "There's been tight security on the boundaries all night."

Joe's knees cracked as he got out of the golf cart. "Let's take a look-see."

They walked carefully, avoiding the pristine surface of the green. The trap, sheer sided and filled with raked white sand, was a dangerous snare for anyone unwise enough to hit to the left of the fourth hole.

"Is it a log?" said the assistant as they approached.

Joe stopped at the edge of the bunker, his hands on his hips. "Hell. It's a body."

She lay as though resting, but the blood that had soaked into the sand under her head destroyed the illusion. She wore casual cream slacks and a simple pale green top. A jacket, neatly folded, had been left beside the body. A golf club, seeming to have been casually flung down, rested near the curled fingers of her right hand.

Joe didn't step onto the smooth sand, but crouched down where he was, eyes narrowed. After a close inspection he said, "She's dead." He sounded more disgusted than upset.

Straightening, he added, "God knows what this will do to the tournament schedule."

CHAPTER ONE

A seagull, riding the wind from the sea, banked over the edge of the golf course in a graceful curve. Although still early in the day, the late summer sun had a bite, and the police officers fanning out in a search pattern from the fourth-hole green welcomed the cooler current of air.

"Who's in charge here?"

Sergeant Mark Bourke blocked the sleekly groomed woman before she could break the cordon of fluttering police tape. With her high-beaked nose, artfully tousled streaked-blond hair, and autocratic manner, she rather reminded Bourke of a pedigreed Afghan hound.

His voice as pleasant as his blunt-featured face, he said, "This area of the course is closed."

Considerably shorter than he, she glared at him, then took a step back, and looked him up and down. Even with a stiff breeze coming up off the ocean, not a strand of her hair moved. Her face was perfectly made up, and her champagne-colored suit was obviously expensive, as was the pale, ruffled silk blouse.

Incongruously, she'd teamed her outfit with white-and-tan laced shoes.

Seeing Bourke glance in the direction of her feet, she said, "Preserving the integrity of a world-class golf course, particularly the surface of the greens, is of the highest priority. High heels would do irreparable damage."

She shot a cold look in the direction of the group clustered around the bunker, then made a sweep of her arm to include the officers searching the surrounding areas. "It's a great pity that you cops don't take such things into account. I was just in time to stop one of your people actually attempting to drive a car onto the course. I told him, carry up anything you need. I'm willing to arrange for you to have an electric cart if necessary. Whatever, just make sure you stick to the marked paths."

The woman put a hand on the tape, clearly intending to enter the delineated site.

"I'm sorry," Bourke said. "You can't come in."

"You can't close this area to me. I own the whole bloody country club. Got that straight? Now, unless you're the boss cocky, get out of my way."

Bourke's agreeable expression didn't change. "This is a crime scene, Ms. Whitlew."

She didn't acknowledge that he knew her name—with her level of public recognition it would have been a surprise if he didn't. Her militant expression dissolved into a smile so charming that he blinked. She asked, thin eyebrows arched, "And you are?"

"Detective Sergeant Mark Bourke."

"Please call me Gussie, Mark. If you know anything about me, you must realize that I don't believe in formality where names are concerned."

Gesturing at the activity inside the taped area, she went on. "No doubt you know I have a very important golf tournament to run, and the longer your people are here, the more damage they do to this green, let alone the rest of the course."

"I'm afraid it's necessary. There's been a death."

She seemed amused at Bourke's delicacy. "A death? How polite. I was told it was some woman with her skull split open." She consulted her diamond-and-gold watch. "The first player in the Whitlew Challenge tees off at ten o'clock, but my greenskeepers need to check this hole out before then, in order to repair the damage you've done."

Unperturbed, Bourke said, "I know it's inconvenient, Ms. Whitlew, but this area will be off-limits for some considerable time."

"That's not acceptable," she snapped. "The tournament is being televised both here and overseas. The Whitlew Challenge is a premier golf tournament for the best women players in the world, and these broadcast commitments must be honored."

"Then the tournament will have to be played without this hole."

Gussie Whitlew shook herself, as though physically repelling Bourke's words. "I need to speak to someone with authority."

"That would be me."

A sudden smile tugged at the corner of Gussie Whitlew's scarlet mouth. "Well, well, well," she said, "if it isn't Detective Inspector Carol Ashton, in the flesh. I've followed your career with interest, Inspector. Great interest."

"Ms. Whitlew. How may I help you?"

Head on one side, Gussie Whitlew was inspecting Carol Ashton's outfit—slacks and a camel blazer. Gussie clicked her tongue. "Not my line of casual wear," she said. "Whose? Peter Bund's, or little Pattie Hart's?"

"I've no idea."

Bourke smiled at Gussie's scandalized reaction to Carol's offhand statement. "No idea? You don't know which label you're wearing?"

"I'm afraid not."

"Then I'll have to take you in hand, my dear. For one thing, those colors you're wearing are not the best choice to enhance your skin tones and blond hair. And your eyes—green are they?"

"This is a crime scene," said Carol with a wry smile, "so, not surprisingly, I didn't dress for a social occasion."

Ignoring this comment, Gussie Whitlew went on. "My makeovers are justly famous. And you may have my services for no charge. What do you say?"

"It's an offer most might find hard to refuse," said Carol, "but I'm afraid I must. Now, Ms. Whitlew, is there a problem?"

"I've just been explaining to your sergeant here that the Whitlew Challenge Tournament is scheduled to begin shortly, and I need this hole cleared and repaired. I'm sure you have the authority to hurry things along, don't you?"

"It's a case of apparent murder. Our investigations can't be hurried along."

Seeming startled, Gussie said, "Murder? I took it to be some accident, or natural causes—if excessive drinking and drugs can be categorized as natural. There are down-and-outers living in the adjoining wildlife reserve in squalid little tents or whatever. God knows I've called the authorities often enough to get them moved on. I presumed it was one of those people."

"It's not likely. The victim's a young woman, and the jacket we found lying beside her has the Whitlew label in it."

"My label? Are you sure?"

"Yes. The jacket's pale green with a faint dark blue stripe."

Her face suddenly blank, Gussie said, "I'd like to see the body."

"I must ask you to keep confidential any details at all about this death."

Gussie flicked her fingers in an impatient gesture. "Of course—that goes without saying."

Carol nodded to Bourke, who raised the tape so Gussie could pass through. "It's not a pleasant sight," Carol warned.

"I've lived an interesting life," said Gussie, "and not always a pleasant one. I think I can take it."

She marched toward the bunker, shoulders back, but Carol observed that she paled noticeably when they approached the edge.

Gesturing for the scene-of-crime technicians to move away from the corpse, Carol said, "Do you recognize her?"

The body lay in the middle of the oval bunker, arms by its sides, palms up in a bizarrely welcoming gesture. The head was tilted to the right, as though the half-open eyes were examining the dark blood staining the white sand.

Bourke put out an arm to steady Gussie Whitlew when she seemed to wilt. "It's Fiona Hawk," she gasped.

Rallying, she added, "A nasty woman, but a wonderful golfer. She's leading the tournament at the moment."

The weight of what she'd said struck her. "Bloody hell. Fiona's leading the tournament—and she's dead."

CHAPTER TWO

"Quite a drop," said Bourke, joining Carol at the waist-high fence that protected spectators from plummeting down the crumbling sandstone cliff to the wet rocks below. The sea was quiet, breaking politely on the tumbled boulders that littered the rock shelf.

"Presuming it's murder," said Carol, "why not throw her over, and hope it looked like an accident?"

"Panic?" said Bourke. "The perp whacks her one, then runs?" He looked back over his shoulder to where the body was being zipped into a bag. "Or maybe the scene was set up as a deliberate tableau, with the arrangement of the golf club and the folded jacket."

"I'd venture it was probably someone who plays golf," said Carol. "The person had the appropriate club for the situation—a sand wedge."

Bourke and Carol followed the stretcher down the final, steep path as the body was carried to the waiting ambulance. From the elevation Carol could see that anxious spectators, looking for the perfect place to view the golfing action, were already streaming onto the course.

It was a beautiful summer morning, singing with golden warmth, and the sweep of the rolling green expanse—embellished by the careful placement of trees, several small lakes, and a meandering stream—was a balm to the eyes. When she looked to the right, the cliffs dropped away to an expanse of dark blue ocean, stretching to meet pale blue sky at the far horizon.

Carol took a deep breath. It was wonderful to be alive, to feel the breeze against her face, to have her muscles move smoothly at her command. To truly appreciate how fortunate she was. She looked at the body bag containing the mortal remains of a young woman who would never again sweat in the sun, stretch her muscles, feel joy or despair.

Someone had attacked with vicious force, and had left her lying inert under the cold light of the stars and moon, oblivious forever to the pounding of the ocean at the foot of the cliff, the night noises of small insects, the sigh of the wind.

Who was there with you? Who struck you with such force that your skull was shattered?

The police doctor's educated guess was that the body had been there for at least eight hours, perhaps more. The cause of death appeared to be a severe head injury, but this would be confirmed by the postmortem.

Carol looked back toward the bunker, where, guarded by two uniformed officers, a small team of scene-of-crime technicians was left to sift the sand and examine the surrounding areas with minute attention. The golf club found with the body and two sand-trap rakes, one of which had almost certainly been used to smooth the sand in the bunker and remove any trace of anyone else's presence, were, with the striped jacket, already on their way to the lab for analysis. The general search of the course had found nothing more, and Carol doubted that even the skills of the SOC people still working at the scene would turn up anything else.

A web of pathways connected the different holes of the course. The one they were on led directly to a far corner of the clubhouse parking area. Local police had been instructed to cordon off that section so that the body could be removed without the interference of sensation-seeking onlookers or the close attention of reporters and TV crews.

Carol was well aware that when the name of the victim was released, a media storm would occur, with overseas outlets carrying the story and quite possibly flying in personnel to cover it. This would not be solely because Fiona Hawk was an international sports star—although Carol had noticed that it was common for sporting personalities to garner particularly intense coverage—but also because Gussie Whitlew was involved.

Immensely rich, and internationally known for her Whitlew line of clothing, Gussie Whitlew had the time and money to indulge her passions, and one of them was golf. The other, as gossip had it, was women. The Whitlew Challenge Golf Tournament brought these two interests together. Some of the best female golfers in the world had been induced to sign on for the invitation-only tournament. Gussie Whitlew was paying generous appearance money, supplying rental cars or, if preferred, limousines with drivers, and picking up hotel bills for luxury accommodation. On top of that was the lure of the first prize, a purse of $1.5 million in U.S. currency.

As Carol and Bourke followed the sweating stretcher-bearers off the course, she saw that some persistent onlookers, though kept at a distance by strategically parked police vehicles and the admonitions of a couple of junior constables, had collected to view whatever it was that had occasioned so considerable a police presence. A photographer Carol recognized with a frown was taking shots. Someone who looked like a cadet reporter was scribbling notes, but most of the others seemed to be trading misinformation or gawking at the stretcher with its ominously covered load.

There was a knot of police officers near the ambulance, and as Carol and Bourke approached someone broke away to stride over to block Carol's way. He was a short, dapper, tweed-jacketed man who demanded in a loud, braying voice, "They say you're in charge. Is that so? Answer me, please."

His accent was upper-class English, and his manner just short of rude. He had thinning white hair, a white mustache, and the rough, ruddy skin of someone who had spent a great deal of time outdoors in harsh weather.

Bourke, immediately alert, had moved to Carol's side. "Sir? Who are you?"

The man, eyes fixed on Carol, paid no attention to Bourke's question. "I'm being obstructed," he declared. "My questions left unanswered." He turned and gestured at the ambulance, where the stretcher was being maneuvered into the back of the vehicle. "Is that my daughter? Gussie Whitlew wouldn't say one way or the other, but I could tell from her manner something was dreadfully wrong."

A stocky, sullen man with a square head, a local detective, named Vernon Coop, whom Carol vaguely knew, strolled over to them. "Inspector Ashton, this is Major Willoughby Hawk. His daughter didn't return to their hotel last night…" He let his voice trail off, his expression clearly indicating that he wasn't anxious to be the source of the coming bad news.

"When did you last see your daughter, Major Hawk?"

This time the major responded to Bourke's question with a dismissive grunt. His attention exclusively to Carol, he barked, "Ashton, is it? If it's a woman's body you've got there, I want to see for myself. I can't believe it's Fiona, but—"

His voice broke. He cleared his throat, and went on. "Didn't realize she hadn't come back to the hotel until I went to her room this morning. Persuaded myself she'd left early for the course, but I knew something was amiss. Bed hadn't been slept in, you see."

Knowing from experience how the bereaved could react to a viewing of a relative's body, Carol said quietly, "Major Hawk, perhaps it would be better if you waited until—"

"I have no intention of waiting. And don't worry about me fainting or anything like that. I'm a military man. Seen my share of death."

"Very well." Carol nodded to Bourke, who went to instruct the two men waiting by the open doors of the ambulance to slide the stretcher out of the vehicle so the body's face could be viewed. A murmur broke from the avid crowd.

The major strutted after Bourke, his head back. He should have looked ridiculous, Carol thought, but instead he gave the impression of stoic bravery. Aware of the onlookers' eager eyes, Carol made sure the major's back was to the crowd and that the body was at least partially shielded by the open rear door of the ambulance.

She was on one side of Major Hawk, with Bourke on the other. Both were ready, if necessary, to physically support the man if his legs gave out. Presuming that Gussie Whitlew's identification had been correct, he was about to receive the shock no parent should ever have to suffer—the confirmed death of a child.

Bourke zipped open the body bag, and the sun shone for the last time on the woman's face. Her short auburn hair was a flare of life next to the pallor of her skin and her slack jaw. Because of the position of the body overnight, postmortem lividity, caused by blood settling to the lowest points of the corpse, had not stained her face.

Major Hawk said nothing at all, but a sigh escaped his lips. He extended trembling fingers, but Bourke took his arm before he could touch the pallid cheek. He turned away, put a hand to his eyes for a moment, then said in an unsteady voice, "It's Fiona. My daughter. What happened to her? Why is she dead?"

"Yesterday—when did you last see her?"

"See her?" he repeated to Carol, his manner distracted. "See Fiona?"

"I know it's been a terrible shock, Major Hawk, but we have to ask questions. You understand that."

He licked his lips, then, clearly making an effort, he said to Carol, "After the day's play was over, Gussie threw a reception in the clubhouse. Fiona—all the golfing ladies were there. Caddies, agents, hangers-on, too. Everyone to do with the tournament."

He seemed stalled at that point, so Carol said, "This must be hard for you."

The major nodded slowly. "I still can't believe it." He straightened his shoulders. "I talked to Fiona for a while, but some photographer wanted some pictures and I had some friends to meet, so I left."

"About what time?"

"Six, or maybe a bit later." His face creased with pain, he choked out, "It was the last time I saw Fiona alive."

Carol and Bourke looked at each other over the little man's bowed head. Carol said, "Major Hawk, Detective Sergeant Bourke will drive you back to your hotel. He'll fill you in with all we know at the present time."

She gestured for a local officer to accompany Hawk to the car, then took Bourke aside. "Treat him gently, of course, Mark, but find out everything you can. Then go back to headquarters and start a full background check on Fiona Hawk, Gussie Whitlew, and anyone else with a high profile who's involved in the tournament. I'll start in the clubhouse with Gussie Whitlew and take it from there."

Bourke gave her a sly grin. "Rather you than me. And watch out, she *has* promised you one of her famous makeovers." He cocked his head. "I can just see you in one of those colorful, flappy things she designs."

"Your imagination's better than mine."

Bourke looked over her shoulder. "And here the lady comes, herself. I'll leave her to you."

Gussie Whitlew was approaching with a daunting expression of fixed determination. Even before she reached Carol she was saying, "Is the fourth hole clear for use? I have my head greenskeeper standing by."

Carol said mildly, "I'm sorry, Ms. Whitlew, but the area where the body was found must remain closed, and later today divers will search the water hazards on the course."

"Divers? During tournament play!"

Repressing a smile at the tone of astonished outrage, Carol said, "I assure you we'll avoid interfering with the tournament play."

"This is all terribly inconvenient, Inspector! I've had my staff working frantically to find some way of making up for the loss of the fourth hole, but the logistics are nearly impossible. We simply must have the full eighteen holes for today's play." She stared at Carol with an expression that nicely mingled entreaty and demand.

Unmoved, Carol said, "As you know, this appears to be a case of murder. It's vital that all evidence be collected from the site."

Her subtle emphasis of the word *murder* didn't have the desired effect. Hands on hips, Gussie Whitlew gave an irritated click of her tongue. "I'm very aware that you have a job to do, but as I explained to your sergeant in some detail, the Whitlew Challenge is an international tournament with top women golfers from around the world. Do you realize the predicament you place me in?" Her tone made it clear she considered the blame for this rested entirely with the police, and, most particularly, Carol's intransigence.

"It may be possible to release the area in time for play tomorrow."

Not at all mollified, Gussie said, "That will be some help, I suppose—if it occurs. As for today, you're forcing me to have the first hole played twice, at the beginning of the day and then again at the end. It's the only solution I can find, and it's a nightmare as far as television coverage and crowd control are concerned."

She paused, apparently waiting for Carol to either apologize or to commiserate with these difficulties.

When no response was forthcoming, she frowned darkly, and went on. "There is one other matter of great importance. I really must insist that the players not be interviewed before the round today. Your detectives have been asking my staff questions, and there's tension enough in the locker room, what with the rumors flying around. On top of that, we're already running late teeing off with the early players. This is being televised, I'll remind you, and I'll have a disaster on my hands if everything doesn't run to schedule. As it is, even though it's a small, select group of sportswomen, I'm still going to be forced to put the early players in groups of four, just to move them fast around the course and make up the time we've lost."

She tilted her chin, glowering at Carol with the air of one who did not expect opposition to her request.

"It's vital, Ms. Whitlew, that everybody who may have helpful information is interviewed immediately, before any contamination of their recollections can take place."

Gussie threw up her hands in a gesture of disgust. "Very well. If you'll excuse me, I'll try and salvage something from this debacle."

As she hurried off, Vernon Coop came over. "So the victim's Fiona Hawk, is it?" he said. "I don't follow golf much, but I know her. Shame. She was a looker, all right."

Carol surveyed Coop, remembering how they'd once met at a conference on community policing. He was the kind of cop that put her teeth on edge. He had a swagger to his bulky body, a superior twist to his thick lips. He was the sort to put the boot into a suspect, then righteously claim that the person had been resisting arrest. And he'd barely escaped with his job over charges of demanding protection money from prostitutes— charges that were dropped when prospective witnesses developed collective amnesia.

"Any sign of rape?" he asked, hands in pockets, feet spread wide. "Up there, alone on the headland, she wouldn't have had a chance."

Carol narrowed her eyes, thinking that Vernon Coop was enjoying the scenario he was painting. "It doesn't look like a sexual attack," she said briskly. "Now, you've got a door-knock going?"

"Too right—going door-to-door in all the streets around here. I reckon nothing will turn up, though. Better chance with the bunch of homeless characters squatting in the reserve next to the golf course." He put up a hand to rub the back of his neck. "You know the routine—we get complaints, we move the bastards, and a few days later, they're bloody well back."

"Ms. Whitlew did mention them."

Coop gave an unamused laugh. "I bet she did! She's the one that does most of the complaining. Anyway, I've got some of my people rounding them up and asking a lot of hard questions. If any of that lot have anything to do with this, I'd say we'll know for sure by the end of the day."

It was difficult for Carol to share this optimism. "I suppose it isn't impossible, but I find it hard to imagine circumstances where Fiona Hawk could meet up with one of these homeless people. There's tight security on the entrance road to the course, and I gather there are patrols on the boundaries from the early evening throughout the night."

"Patrols? Yeah, sure," said Coop, contemptuous. "Amateurs. Drive around a bit, stop for coffee, maybe have a snooze for a while. *Cushy* is the word for it."

"Any of your cops doing it as a second job?"

Carol's question obviously took him back. After a thoughtful pause he said, "Maybe. I'll get back to you on that."

As Carol turned to go, he said, "Don't suppose you read the sports pages much, eh?"

"If you're asking if I follow golf closely, the answer's no. Why are you asking?"

"You won't get *me* paying much attention to women's sport, but I certainly noticed Fiona Hawk. A real looker, and sexy as hell."

Not bothering to hide her impatience, Carol said, "So?"

"She might have looked great, but Fiona could be a bit of a bitch." When Carol raised her eyebrows, he went on. "Like, she was suing her agent for God knows how much money. She claims he's been screwing her for years." His suggestive smile widened. "Not that Fiona minded a bit of screwing herself, if you can believe what you hear. And by the look of her, I'd say it's true. Story goes, she had the hots for just about anything in pants."

He waited to see if Carol had any response, then said, "So you'd better wish on your lucky stars that some squatter from the camp *did* do her in." A meaningful look was followed by, "Otherwise, I'd say you're in for a load of trouble. A shitload."

CHAPTER THREE

The clubhouse building was like nothing Carol had ever seen on a golf course before, but then most of her prior experience had been years ago, when she had played occasional games on public golf courses where the facilities had been strictly utilitarian.

This clubhouse shrieked for attention: Its sleek white curves, the curling sweep of its defiantly red metal roof, the glittering chrome entrance doors, and huge oval picture windows made for a structure that looked defiantly out of place, as though some futuristic private mansion had been picked up and plopped down on the golf course.

There was much activity, with people moving quickly in and out the huge chrome entry doors, and vehicles jockeying for position in the crowded parking area. A broadcast van, dish turned to the sky, was hogging two prized spaces near the entrance, and Carol was irritated to notice that a handheld TV camera was pointed her way.

She'd given strict instructions to Vernon Coop to use his local officers to keep television cameras as far away as possible, but this particular team was here for the tournament, and so couldn't be told to move.

Gussie Whitlew intercepted Carol before she reached the shallow marble steps of the clubhouse. She'd changed her golf shoes for high heels, but even with this advantage, she was still a head shorter than Carol. "About Willoughby Hawk—he came asking me if I'd seen Fiona, but I couldn't bring myself to tell him."

Carol said, "There's a television camera trained on us. I can't see a microphone, but that doesn't mean they aren't picking up our voices."

Gussie glanced in the direction of the TV van, "I wouldn't have thought you were shy about publicity, Inspector Ashton. I see you on television often enough."

"That's because some of my cases have been high-profile ones. I certainly don't seek media exposure."

"Ah," said Gussie. "My credo is that any publicity is good publicity." Seeing Carol glance back at the broadcast van, she added, "Perhaps we had better discuss something innocuous. What do you think of my clubhouse? I told my architect I wanted something very different."

"I can see that."

Gussie grinned at Carol's dry tone. "I do things differently," she said. "Always have. Always will. Come on in and see the inside decor. I'm very proud of it."

The reception area was filled with a crowd of people, all apparently determined to talk at the top of their voices. Waiters carrying red trays negotiated the crush, dispensing coffee, mineral water, and a selection of finger foods.

The building's outside theme of white walls, much glass, and gleaming metal was repeated. The whole area was carpeted in plush dark red, with the scattered lounge chairs upholstered in a lighter but matching shade.

A large fountain—in the form of a stylized female golfer at the top of her swing—dominated the center of the area.

Water spurted from the head of her club and showered over her gleaming chrome form, splashing into a red metal circular pool—the color blending with the carpet—where the water was agitated into white foam.

"Quite something, don't you think?" asked Gussie, indicating the fountain with a proprietary gesture. "The inspiration for it was mine, but the artist added her own little touches."

"It's certainly eye-catching."

Gussie chuckled. "I can tell you're impressed."

Over the reception desk a huge white banner with red letters proclaimed INAUGURAL WHITLEW CHALLENGE GOLF TOURNAMENT. Below it, the reception desk, shaped like a transparent, curving plastic wave, was staffed by a team of young women, each wearing a formfitting tailored black jacket and deep red slacks that were the same color as the carpet.

"I admire your color coordination," said Carol.

Gussie grinned at her dry tone. "It took a lot of doing. You can have no idea how difficult it is to match carpet, upholstery, and clothing, although the main problem was the trays the waiters have. I had a hell of a time getting just the right shade."

"Inspector?"

Carol acknowledged Anne Newsome, whom she'd sent with Terry Roham to make preliminary inquiries of the clubhouse and course staff, then said to Gussie Whitlew, "Have you met Detective Constable Newsome, Ms. Whitlew?"

"You're going to have to call me Gussie, Inspector Ashton. Formality bores me." She added with a sardonic lift of an eyebrow, "However, naturally I fully intend to treat *you* with the proper respect and to use your formal title. And yes, I have met Detective Newsome."

Gussie favored the young constable with an appreciative smile. "Indeed, she asked me some very searching questions."

The warmth of this appreciation caused Carol to wonder if she should warn Anne of Gussie's reportedly enthusiastic appetite for her own sex, but a look at Anne's amused expression convinced her that it wasn't necessary.

Carol could clearly see why Gussie Whitlew might find Anne Newsome of interest. Her curly brown hair and olive skin glowed with health, she moved with energy and grace, and in the time she'd been in Carol's department she'd lost weight and gained assurance.

Gussie's expression changed as she caught sight of someone in the crowded reception area. "Davy, over here."

In obedience to her command, an almost-handsome man with short, bleached yellow-white hair, contrasting with his deep tan, black leather pants, and tight white sleeveless top that showed off his impressively muscled chest, came to her side.

Towering over her diminutive figure, he said without much interest, "Yes, Gussie, what can I do for you?"

"My assistant, Davy Vere," said Gussie, looking up at him approvingly. "Davy's my right-hand man. He knows where the bodies are buried, don't you, Davy?"

He inclined his head. "If you say so." He had a soft voice with a faintly insolent tone—a tone, Carol thought, that went well with his disdainful expression.

After introducing Carol—Anne Newsome had already met him—Gussie said, "Inspector Ashton needs privacy to continue her inquiries." She gave Carol an ironic smile. "I am getting the lingo right? *Continuing your inquiries* sounds so harmless, doesn't it? But of course you're trying to trap someone in a lie, aren't you?"

Carol lifted her shoulders in an infinitesimal shrug. "It's my job."

Davy made a noise deep in his throat that Carol took to mean either disapproval or contempt. Looking at his expression, she decided *derision* was a better choice, and made a mental note to have Davy Vere checked out for prior offenses.

"So, Davy, I think my office would be the place for the Inspector, don't you?"

Davy looked at his employer with disapproval. "No, I don't. You'll be needing it later."

Gussie laughed. "Do forgive Davy. He can be so blunt at times." Her amusement faded. "Please clear my desk. We'll be along in a moment."

He gave a quick nod, then strode off. "Like a beautiful animal, isn't he?" said Gussie.

Carol saw Anne Newsome's lips twitch. She repressed a smile herself, asking, "How long has Mr. Vere been working for you?"

"Years. When he first came to me, he fancied himself a designer, but he has no real talent in that area. Eventually he became my assistant, with all that entails."

"Which is?"

"A very handsome salary, demanding responsibilities and, because he speaks for me, a great deal of power. Money talks, as they say, and a great deal of money talks very loudly."

As she was saying this, a woman approached to say, "Excuse me, Gussie, but I have a little problem."

"Kasha! If you have *any* problem, small or large, I'm here to solve it." Turning to Carol and Anne, she went on, "May I introduce one of golf's premier players, Kasha London."

While the introductions were completed, Carol appraised the woman. Kasha London was Carol's height but had a heavier build. She had a pleasant, open expression and a warm, friendly manner. Her clothing, all in neutral colors, blended with her brown hair and lightly tanned skin. The only really striking thing about her was her voice, which was deep and musical.

"Now, Kasha," said Gussie with the air of one who had a solution for everything, "what's the problem?"

"I believe someone's been through my things in the locker room."

Her astonishment obvious, Gussie said, "Are you sure, Kasha? My staff have been very strictly screened. I'd be shocked if any of them were involved in such a thing. Is something missing?"

Kasha seemed embarrassed to be causing this concern. "It's probably nothing, Gussie. I just had the impression that someone had moved my things around. There's nothing missing that I can see, but I only had a quick look when I came in this morning."

Gussie was reassuring. "I'll get Davy on it right away."

Watching Kasha make her way across the crowded reception area, she said to Carol, "See? Nobody recognizes her. It's not good enough to be a champion; you have to have charisma, presence. Rather like you, Inspector."

A flash of light caught Carol's attention. The photographer she had seen in the parking area was using a bulky professional camera to take group photographs. Carol said, "Hilary O'Dell."

"From your tone," said Gussie, "I gather you are not altogether a fan of Hilary's. She's a fine celebrity photographer. I've employed her for the duration of the tournament."

"On many occasions she's harassed her subjects," said Carol, watching the woman move from group to group. Most people seemed more than willing to pose, and the photographer was animated, chatting to them as she organized the shots.

She had thick, brassy hair secured in a ponytail, strong, hawklike features, and a full-lipped mouth that stretched widely when she smiled, which she did constantly, revealing a set of excellent teeth.

With irritation, Carol realized that Hilary O'Dell was moving in their direction. Hoping to avoid her, Carol said to Gussie, "Would you mind if we went to your office now?"

"Detective Inspector Carol Ashton," said Hilary O'Dell, pushing her way roughly through intervening people. Her voice was not friendly. "You're here on official business, I imagine." She swung up her camera.

Carol said, "No comment, and no photographs—" She threw a quick glance to Anne Newsome, who moved to a position where she could take action if necessary.

"Oh, please," Gussie protested, putting a hand on Carol's arm. "Reconsider, Inspector. I'd be honored to be photographed with you. I'm publishing a Whitlew Challenge commemorative book as a permanent photographic record of the tournament. I'd be so delighted to present you with an autographed, leather-bound edition."

Carol repeated to Hilary O'Dell, "No photographs." When the photographer, frowning, lowered her camera, Carol said to Gussie, "May we go, now?"

"Keep snapping," Gussie instructed the photographer. "As many big names as you can get."

She set off, leading Carol and Anne through the crowd toward the reception desk. Over her shoulder she said to Carol, "I could feel a chill in the air. I gather you and Hilary have some history?"

"We've run into each other before." Carol wasn't going to elaborate. She'd had Hilary O'Dell detained on two occasions, and been tempted to do the same on several other cases where the photographer had stepped over the bounds of professionalism and impeded Carol's investigations. And, apart from that, she had to admit to herself there was a strictly personal reason to dislike the woman.

As they moved through the crowd, Carol listened to snatches of conversation, wondering if Fiona Hawk's death had yet become common knowledge. She much preferred to interview people who were unaware of any details of a crime, but it was difficult to keep information under wraps—all it needed was a cop big-noting, or someone on Gussie Whitlew's staff passing on the word—and the news would spread like wildfire.

Someone recognized her: "Isn't that Carol Ashton? What's *she* doing here?" Another person made reference to an accident: "I think someone's fallen off the cliff. There's an ambulance and cops everywhere." Most of the conversations, however, seemed exclusively on the subject of golf—the state of the course, the Whitlew Challenge itself, and comments on the various players' chances at pulling off a top-three placement.

The din faded as they entered the thickly carpeted corridor leading to the management offices. Davy Vere was still putting material away in an office that was no bigger than the others. Carol had fully expected that Gussie's personal office would be grandiose, but it was only of medium size. An attractive room, it had iron-gray carpeting and soft rose walls, and the desk was clearly an expensive antique, but otherwise it was obviously a working office. There were no decorative touches, and no photographs or paintings. A bank of screens was set into one wall. The sound was off, but images of the golf course were displayed. The central, and larger, screen was showing a series of short clips of players making difficult shots.

Seeing Anne examining the screens, Gussie said, "Direct feed from the broadcast truck. I insist on it." She pointed to the larger screen. "That's how they're making up for the late start—a rehash of yesterday's play."

The picture was showing a player hitting a ball out of a bunker in a shower of sand—a beautiful shot that had the ball coming to rest almost against the flagpole in the hole. "Isn't that Fiona Hawk?" said Carol.

Gussie shook her head morosely. "She finished yesterday eight under par, leading by three strokes."

"Followed by?"

This amused Gussie. "Aha! You think she was bumped off so someone else could win? A bit farfetched, I'm afraid. It's a four-day tournament, so anything can happen, but if you want to know, at five under par there was one person—Kasha London, whom you met. Bit of a fluke, that, as she's a good, but not sensational, golfer. Then behind two shots back were two tied for third—the Aussie, Brinella Altunga, and the Yank, Toni Karstares."

Carol, who didn't follow golf closely, nevertheless knew both these last names. Brinella Altunga was a young Aboriginal golfer who'd learned the sport on a rough, little nine-hole course in the middle of nowhere. She'd had the good fortune to be mentored by an established male player, who'd seen to it that she had every opportunity to succeed—and she had in spectacular fashion.

Toni Karstares had caused much angst in the professional ranks of woman golfers by being defiantly, and vocally, out of the closet. She answered any question about her sexual preference with matter-of-fact frankness, although—sigh of relief from the golfing authorities—she drew the line at outing anyone else.

Davy Vere, who'd been transferring folders and documents from the desktop to a large, cream floor safe, slammed it shut, spun the dial, then swung around to say to Gussie, "I've ordered refreshments for your guests." There was a disapproving edge to this last word. He added, "Anything else?"

"Double-check that the changes to the tournament have been implemented, and make sure the TV commentators have got it straight. I want to hear them saying what I want them to say. Hurry, the first players will be teeing off any minute now. And one more thing—Kasha London thinks someone'd been through her locker. When you have time, check that out, will you?"

Davy gave another of his quick nods and left the room, giving Anne a quick up-and-down look as he went.

"He's bi." Gussie's tone was helpful. "If you fancy him, you should know that."

Anne's lips curved in a slight smile. "Thank you for the information."

Carol, her tone all business, said, "We'll be questioning everyone who might have seen Fiona Hawk in the hours before her death. There was some sort of function here in the clubhouse yesterday, wasn't there?"

Obviously riled, Gussie said, "Not *some* sort of function— it was an absolutely first-class one, catered at the highest level. After the first day's play of what I fully expect will become an annual and highly regarded event, I put on a reception to officially welcome the players. It was a strictly informal affair as far as dress was concerned—I certainly didn't expect professional sportswomen to lug full formal gear with them to the course on the first day of the Challenge."

"Who was there, apart from the players?"

"It was almost entirely a PR exercise, of course, but everyone who's anyone in the Aussie golfing world was there, plus quite a few important people from the States and Britain There were a few obligatory celebrities, and players' agents, managers, sponsors, whatever. And, of necessity, representatives of the media."

She grimaced a little at the word *media*. Carol was well aware that Gussie Whitlew had a love-hate relationship with the media, pandering to them shamelessly when she had a fashion line to sell or when she detected an opportunity for self-promotion. It was quite another thing when probing questions were asked about her private life, or comments made about her close relationships with political figures who might be expected to frame legislation favoring her fashion company.

A knock at the door elicited Gussie's barked command to enter. The waiter was laden with a red tray carrying an assortment of canapés, exquisite china cups, and a matching coffeepot.

"I'll have to leave you in a moment," said Gussie, gesturing to the waiter to put the tray down on the desk. She waved him out of the room as she said, "Davy may be good, but some details need my personal touch. But before I go, you still haven't told me how Willoughby took the news."

This seemed an odd question to Carol, as surely Gussie Whitlew would expect the man to be upset. "He seemed very shaken," she said. "He asked to see the body, and confirmed it was his daughter. I arranged for him to be taken back to his hotel."

"I'm not surprised he was upset, because now his good life stops."

"In what way?"

Gussie pursed her lips. "Frankly, I think it was over for Willoughby anyhow. They haven't been getting on, at least not lately. He's been traveling around with Fiona since her career took off. Called himself her manager, but that was a laugh, and everyone knew it. More a freeloader, I'd say, sponging off his daughter. Recently Fiona accused her father of getting too cozy with her agent, Ralph Syncomm."

"She was suing her agent, wasn't she?"

"Very good," said Gussie, eyebrows arched. "You do move fast, Inspector. Fiona was convinced Ralph was swindling her, and she thought Willoughby was helping him. She confided in me that she was going to ruin Ralph and dump her father."

"When was this?"

"I don't know. In the last day or so. I had a lot of financial matters to discuss with the players, especially Fiona, as she is—was—one of the brightest stars in women's golf."

Gussie chuckled. "I don't want to do your work for you, Inspector, but I'd say there's a motive for murder, right there. Don't you agree?"

CHAPTER FOUR

"Well, Kerrie-Louise, here we are at one of the most beautiful golf courses in the country—perhaps the world. Recently redesigned—no, make that entirely rebuilt—by famed golf course architect Binnie Bayline."

The view on the monitor switched to a smoothly attractive woman with a perfect set of white teeth. *"Yes, Gavin, the Whitlew Country Club is in immaculate condition for the second round of the inaugural Whitlew Challenge. We have a wonderful day of golf ahead of us, although the tournament is a little late in starting this morning."*

The camera returned to the male commentator, a severely weather-beaten, somewhat overweight man with wispy brown hair and a bulbous nose. *"Unfortunately the fourth green, due to an unforeseen problem, is out of commission today,"* he said in a hushed and serious tone, *"so the first hole will be played twice, the second time at the end of the round to make up the required eighteen holes."*

Carol glanced up from a map Gussie had provided of the Whitlew Country Club to see Anne Newsome glaring at the screen, muttering to herself, "It really gets to me how a man can look as rough as that, but the woman has to be glam."

"At least she isn't *young* and glam," said Carol.

The next shot showed the announcers side by side. The woman, her expression concerned, said, *"And, Gavin, that isn't the only problem facing the tournament, is it?"*

A closeup emphasized Gavin's grave expression. *"No, Kerrie-Louise, it isn't. This morning we have the bombshell announcement that the leader after the first day's play, famed British golfer Fiona Hawk, has withdrawn from the Whitlew Challenge."*

Anne declared, "The guy even gets the most interesting things to say. Poor old Kerrie-Louise is just there to feed him lines."

The camera cut to Kerrie-Louise, who was looking surprised. *"No reason given, Gavin?"*

"Apparently the police have been at the course since early this morning, but to date no official statement has been made. Now, as play is about to start, let's take a look at the revised leader board..."

As Anne leaned over the desk to punch the mute button on the control panel set into its surface, Carol grinned at her constable's frowning face. "It's no use getting your blood pressure up, Anne. Call the television network or send an e-mail. It's worth it, because companies work on the principle that for every person complaining, there are at least ten who think the same way but don't get around to calling or writing."

Asking Anne to describe her morning's activities, Carol learned that Anne and Terry Roham had compiled a list of people close to the victim—this was incomplete—and had carried out preliminary questioning of the ground staff, the two men on security guard at the entrance gates, and some of the administrative personnel. The kitchen hands and waiters had not been available, nor had the receptionists staffing the entrance area.

"And no one involved in getting the tournament underway was available, and Ms. Whitlew made sure we knew the locker room and media rooms were out of bounds while the radio and TV people were doing interviews."

"From what Gussie Whitlew said before, you asked her some questions too."

Anne grinned. "Well, I tried. Mostly it was Ms. Whitlew announcing what a disaster the whole situation was. She did tell me all about Fiona Hawk's agent, Ralph Syncomm, and what a crook he is. She went into exhaustive detail about sports agents, so now I know rather more about them than I ever intended."

Carol asked for details, thinking as she did so that Gussie seemed to be making pointed efforts to paint both Major Willoughby Hawk and Ralph Syncomm in an unfavorable light.

Anne was reporting on the security at the front entrance— basically neither of the two guards had anything helpful to say, and they kept no specific records of people coming and going— when Davy Vere strode into the room.

"Gussie sent me to show you around." His manner didn't indicate any pleasure in the task, but his expression warmed slightly as he looked at Anne. He said to her, "That guy with you earlier—Rowan, I think his name is—"

"It's Roham," said Anne.

"Whatever. He said to tell you he's interviewing the pool attendant, if you want him."

"Yes, go and find Terry," said Carol to Anne. "Take over whatever he's doing, and send him to liaise with the local police. They're rounding up some homeless people on the adjacent reserve for questioning."

"Jesus," said Davy, "can't you cops leave the poor buggers alone? Just because they choose to live outside society's pathetic idea of what's normal, they get hammered."

"They're potential witnesses, nothing more."

"Yeah? And you'll ask them a few civilized questions, then let them go back to their camp? Not bloody likely."

"The local division has jurisdiction."

His mouth twisted as though he'd tasted something bitter. "Yeah, sure," he said. "Pass it off to someone else. It's easy to wash your hands of anything that makes you uncomfortable."

"Perhaps we can continue this debate while you show me the clubhouse."

He ducked his head and exited without waiting to see if Carol was following him.

"What a sweetheart," said Anne.

Carol grinned. "And I think he likes you."

* * *

Working with cool efficiency, Davy took Carol on a tour of the clubhouse and adjoining buildings. He didn't mention the homeless people again, and gave the briefest possible replies to her questions about the clubhouse. Apart from the management offices, which were comfortable but not overly lavish, the areas intended for players and the public were splendidly appointed.

"I can't show you the interview rooms," he declared. "Gussie's worried a reporter will see you and start asking questions."

Irritated by his curt manner, Carol said acerbically, "It's inevitable that the media will start asking questions. I imagine they are gathering outside the gate right now."

He shrugged. "As long as a reporter doesn't nail you when I'm responsible for you."

Davy arranged for a female attendant to accompany Carol while she viewed the private facilities for the players. Some of the competitors were still changing, or chatting over refreshments in a commodious lounge area. There were deluxe locker rooms, saunas, showers, and associated areas for the pampering attentions of a masseur or beauty specialist. Everything was extremely luxurious and, thinking of the female locker room at police headquarters, Carol shook her head ruefully. Such comparisons, she thought, were more than odious.

"Nice, eh?" said her guide, who had RUTH embroidered on her red uniform. She was a thin, fit-looking woman in her mid-forties. Giving Carol a wry grin, she went on. "Want the little dears to feel they're having special attention."

Knowing how much staff routinely overheard, Carol smiled in turn. "One of the little dears, as you call them, has died. Did you know?"

"Up on the fourth? Yes, everyone has heard about that. Rumor has that it's Fiona Hawk, because she's out of the tournament. That right?"

Sure that this fact would be common knowledge by the afternoon, as news outlets leapt on the story, Carol said, "Yes, it's Fiona Hawk. Did you know her?"

"She threw her weight around, that one. But she was poetry on a golf course and she tipped well, so I personally have got no complaints. How'd she die?"

"I'm afraid I can't discuss that."

Ruth gave a snort of laughter. "Of course you can. You don't want to."

Carol nodded agreeably. "That's right. Do you mind if I ask you a few questions?"

Ruth spread her arms wide. "Ask away."

"I suppose you get to know the players reasonably well."

"Gussie encourages us to be on first-name terms with everybody. Most of the women are fine with that, except for Fiona Hawk, who made it clear on the first day that, as far as she was concerned, we were little better than servants. And Brinella Altunga—she keeps to herself. I don't think I've heard her speak more than a couple of times."

"Perhaps she's shy."

Ruth gave Carol a knowing look. "More likely she's following strict instructions from her brother, Eddie. You met him? He's super protective, and Fiona had quite a bit to say about that."

Carol's attentive expression encouraged Ruth to go on. "Yesterday, before play started, everyone was in here getting ready. Brinella's brother came with her right to the door, and whispered to her before she came in. That was enough for Fiona Hawk. She said it was incestuous, in that hoity-toity English voice of hers that really carried, so that Brinella and everybody else heard what she was saying. Went on about deviants and so on until someone shut her up."

"And who did that?"

"Toni Karstares. Really took a piece out of Fiona. Laid into her, you know, and told her where to get off." It was clear from Ruth's attitude that she heartily approved of this action. "Toni was red in the face, like she'd explode any minute, and I for one wouldn't have been surprised if she had lost it completely and hit Fiona, but Kasha and Beth Shima got hold of Toni and calmed her down."

"And what was Fiona's reaction to this attack from Toni Karstares?"

"She didn't care. Shrugged it off, said something about Toni being queer, and just went on getting ready to play. Brinella, though, was a bit upset. A few tears, that sort of thing. I was surprised when Ashleigh Piddock went over to comfort her, because that kid's the most self-centered young woman I've ever met, and I've met some, I can tell you."

Carol asked a few more questions about the routine in the locker room and the other staff. She was about to leave when Ruth, dropping her voice, said, "Davy Vere out there waiting for you—have you asked him about Fiona Hawk?"

"Should I?"

"He put the hard word on her, and she laughed at him. He didn't like that—he takes himself very seriously, does Davy. Not that I'm saying he would do anything, but he's one of those slow burners, if you know what I mean."

* * *

When Carol went out into the corridor, Davy was standing with a birdlike young woman, whom Carol recognized as one of the staff she'd seen behind the main reception desk.

"Mina says Uta Dahlberg wants to see you." When Carol frowned, Davy said, "She's a sports agent. You'll have to do your homework, Inspector."

He really was obnoxious, Carol thought, wondering how Gussie Whitlew put up with Davy's brand of sullen incivility. "I'll see Ms. Dahlberg now," she said.

Mina took her back to Gussie's office. While she was waiting, her mobile chirped. It was Bourke, back at headquarters. "I got nothing useful out of Major Hawk, because of a combination of alcohol and grief. We can try again later. And another thing—your Aunt Sarah's looking for you. I spoke to her, and she was very mysterious, but she said to tell you she's here in Sydney and staying with Sybil."

"Aunt Sarah didn't tell me she was coming down from the Blue Mountains." Nor, Carol thought, that she would be staying with Sybil, and not with Carol.

Bourke would be running a criminal record check on anyone close to the victim, and Carol asked him to add Davy Vere to the list. They spoke for a few minutes about Major Hawk, ending their conversation when Mina returned to the office with a woman of medium height and build, but with an aura of burning intensity. She had long, black hair and pale skin, and from the moment she entered the room she fixed her dark eyes on Carol with a laser stare.

Carol introduced herself and asked Uta Dahlberg to take a seat. When the woman spoke, she had a light, clear voice, quite in contrast with her coiled-spring demeanor. Carol had also expected that there might be an accent to go with her name, but she sounded quite Australian.

"I asked to see you, Inspector, because I've recently negotiated a contract to represent Fiona Hawk. Gussie now tells me that she is dead. Is that so?"

Carol opened her notebook and picked up her gold pen. "That's so."

A look of consternation crossed Uta Dahlberg's face. "You're sure it's Fiona?"

"Yes."

"It wasn't an accident?"

It would be usual, Carol thought, to assume that a sudden death of a healthy young person *was* an accident. Unless, of course, specific details about the body had already been leaked to the rumor mill. Carol said, "Possibly not."

A slight smile lit Uta Dahlberg's face. "You're not very communicative, Inspector."

Irritated by the possibility that Gussie may have disregarded Carol's request not to give out any details about the body on the headland, Carol said, "Did Gussie Whitlew discuss with you what had happened to Fiona Hawk?"

"She told me Fiona was dead. That's all. Of course I asked Gussie how she'd died, but she shrugged and said that you had instructed her not to say. That's why I asked to see you."

"When did you last see Ms. Hawk?"

This standard question from Carol seemed to amuse her. "Now you're sounding like a real detective," she said.

Carol waited, attentive. Uta Dahlberg's smile faded. "I had a long talk with Fiona during the function last night. She told me that she'd advised Syncomm that he was no longer representing her, and that she would be signing a contract with me."

"Was there still a valid contract between them?"

"Good question. There was still a contract, but Fiona told him that she was unilaterally breaking it, and that if he made any trouble she'd have him charged with fraud, embezzlement—the works."

"I was under the impression she was in the process of suing him, anyway."

Uta shook her head. "It was going to be a long, ugly, and very expensive affair if she went ahead, so Fiona was willing to drop the proceedings if he made restitution, and released her from the contract."

"And Mr. Syncomm's reaction?"

"I've no idea, though I imagine he wasn't happy. He gets twenty percent of Fiona's earnings and, as she's so successful, that's quite a lot of money."

Taking the cap off her gold fountain pen, Carol said, "What time was this conversation you had with her?"

"Quite early, about seven, I'd say. We talked for about a quarter of an hour or so, then Fiona went to play mind games with the players sharing the top of the leader board with her."

"Mind games?"

With what seemed reluctant admiration, Uta Dahlberg said, "I'm afraid Fiona fully subscribed to the philosophy that all's fair in love and war. And every tournament she entered was war to her. That's why I was so keen to represent Fiona—she was a winner. I didn't always approve of her techniques, but they worked. If she had the opportunity, she'd always have a friendly chat with anyone she thought a threat in the competition. She'd studied their golfing games and knew their weaknesses. Her aim was to plant a seed of doubt, undermine confidence just a little, to give her a possible edge the next day."

Reflecting that Fiona Hawk was becoming more and more the perfect murderee, Carol asked, "So she intended to play these mind games with...?"

"Look at the leader board—Kasha, Toni, and Australia's very own Brinella, although in Brinella's case Fiona would know she didn't have a chance, because Eddie, Brinella's brother, is always with her like a guard dog. And I know she was worried about Ashleigh Piddock, who birdied the last three holes and was just behind the frontrunners at two under par."

Carol looked at the notepad where she'd absently doodled interconnecting boxes, each containing an arrow. If Fiona's death had been murder—and she was sure it was—the list of possible suspects seemed to be growing fast. She wondered with an inner, sardonic smile if it wouldn't be easier to establish who *didn't* have a motive rather than who did.

"Would you mind giving me your impression of the players you believe Fiona may have approached?"

Uta appeared pleased to be asked for her opinion. "I represent one of them," she said. "Kasha London. She was one of my first clients, but now she's coming near the end of her competitive career. A nice but unexciting player. I'm sure Gussie can't be happy that Kasha's at the top of the leader board, but that'll only be temporary. It's a shame, but Kasha hasn't won a tournament for several years, so I'm sure she'll fade in this one."

"Looking at the players in this tournament, is there anyone that Fiona Hawk would be particularly worried about?"

"No question—Toni Karstares. She's a dynamo on the course. She's a lesbian, which shouldn't be the first thing people mention, but it is. She'll be pleased Fiona's out of the running. Toni's been runner-up to her twice this year, already."

"And Brinella Altunga?"

Uta made a face. "I'd love to represent her, but her management is strictly a family affair. She'd be a dream to have as a client—sports ambassador for her country, role model for Aboriginal kids, et cetera, et cetera, et cetera. And like I said, Fiona would have trouble getting near to Brinella—her brother would see to that."

Carol scanned the list of tournament competitors Gussie had supplied. "You mentioned Ashleigh Piddock, too."

"Ashleigh Piddock? She's an American teenage sensation, but the single most irritating young woman I've ever met. I represent her, too, by the way."

When Uta Dahlberg had gone, Carol took the opportunity to call Aunt Sarah back. She dialed Sybil's familiar number, and her heart lurched when Sybil answered. "Carol, how nice to hear your voice. I'll get Aunt Sarah for you."

While she waited, Carol pictured her aunt's short, plump form, energetic gestures, and corona of wild white hair.

Aunt Sarah picked up with a blunt statement. "Carol, darling, I thought you should know, I expect to be arrested tomorrow."

CHAPTER FIVE

Calling the pathologist, Jeff Duke, to beg him as a special favor to expedite his postmortem on Fiona Hawk, as usual made him froth and bubble. "Jesus Christ, Carol, you're a pest! You always want everything yesterday, don't you? People are popping off at an alarming rate this week, so I'm up to the eyebrows with bodies."

"Please, Jeff—this is an important one."

He snorted derisively. "You always say that, Carol. All right, as usual I can't resist your charms, but you owe me, big time. Tomorrow morning, early—which I might point out means I'm giving up part of my Saturday, in case you haven't noticed—is the best I can manage. And I don't want Mark Bourke present while I do it; I want *you*."

She agreed without enthusiasm, thinking how many postmortems she'd witnessed and how familiarity had never helped her become nonchalant about seeing a human body gutted.

As she put down the receiver, her attention was caught by the monitor showing the program as it was broadcast from the course. Carol punched up the muted sound to catch commentator Kerrie-Louise saying, "*...inspiration for young sportswomen, and for the Aboriginal race.*"

"*Yes, Kerrie-Louise,*" Gavin agreed, "*in our Whitlew Challenge Player Profile we look at the short but illustrious career of Brinella Altunga.*"

Although familiar with the young Aborigine because of the quantity of media attention she had attracted in the short time she'd been on the professional golf circuit, Carol knew only the standard nonentity-becomes-star story, so she listened closely to the short profile.

The images of Brinella in a series of interview segments showed her as a shy, rather inarticulate person with smooth dark skin, lustrous brown eyes, and the demeanor of one who would rather be somewhere else. The clips of Brinella playing golf were entirely different. As an athlete she had confidence and grace, and a liquid swing that put her in the select group of consistent, accurate long-hitters.

There was a very brief summation of Brinella's life, starting with her early years in a small country town, then the chance introduction to a successful male golfer, which turned out to be the first step in a series of fortunate events that had ultimately led to her spectacular arrival on the international women's circuit, where she had won a major tournament shortly after turning professional.

Carol was interested to see that Brinella was almost always accompanied by her brother, whose principal facial expression suggested simmering resentment. Eddie Altunga was mentioned in the profile as being both Brinella's manager and caddie, plus, as the announcer said with emotion, her inspiration.

The program shifted to a live feed from the course, with Kerrie-Louise announcing that Brinella Altunga was about to putt. "*And over to you, Debbie.*"

"*Thank you, Kerrie-Louise,*" breathed the unseen analyst stationed at the hole. She spoke in the customary half-whisper used to avoid distracting the players. *"And it's a long one for birdie. Note Brinella's careful preshot routine. And she's hit it with authority, and it's…Yes!"*

Muted cheers and clapping were picked up by the microphone. Brinella leaned down and picked her golf ball out of the hole, handing it to her caddie for cleaning. Her brother was on camera for a moment or two, and Carol studied him. He was thin and he held his chin high, his body language, even laden with the golf bag, suggesting defiant bravado.

The picture shifted to another golfer teeing off. *"Kasha London's opted to go with an eight iron on this hole…And she strikes it cleanly."* The camera followed the flight of the ball against the blue sky. *"Looks like the wind's holding that one up,"* declared the announcer. *"She'll be wanting to hug the left side of the fairway… Ah! She's deep in the rough. That placement won't make her happy!"*

Carol glanced at her watch, deciding to check on the crime scene before organizing interviews. The entrance lobby of the clubhouse was now almost empty. Outside, the sun glared down from a cloudless sky, but a stiff breeze from the ocean tempered the heat.

The technicians were in the parking area, packing up. "Find anything startling?" she asked.

"We sieved the whole damn bunker," said the head of the team. He opened the top of a brown paper evidence bag to let Carol look in. "Found what you'd expect—animal droppings, bits of insects, stuff like that. And this."

The *this* was an exquisite gold bracelet, made of fitted flat links.

"The clasp's broken," he said.

"Where was it in relation to the body?"

"Just under the surface of the sand, about a meter from her head, right side."

Taking off her dark glasses, Carol peered closely at the bracelet. "I'll need photographs, blown up."

He nodded. "Fast as we can."

"Is it okay to open up the crime-scene area? The club's anxious to have the hole back for the competition."

He nodded again. "Okay by me, but you're the boss."

In her jacket pocket, Carol's phone trilled. Her junior constable, Terry Roham, sounded cheerful. "I'm at the local cop shop. They're holding one of the vagrants they picked up this morning in the nature reserve, and Coop says maybe you'd like to get over here. He'll send someone to pick you up. Only be five minutes."

"I'll be at the main gate."

After leaving a message for Anne to say where she'd be, Carol strolled to the main gate. The morning's activity around the clubhouse was now relocated to the course. The sound of clapping carried faintly from one of the closer greens, and Carol could see different assemblies of spectators either moving quickly to keep up with the players as they walked to their balls on the fairways or clustered around greens, watching in eager silence to see a putt fall in—or not.

There was activity, however, outside the main entrance. As Carol approached the guardhouse, a little glass-walled edifice between the entrance and exit boom gates, there was a flurry of movement in the small crowd lined up along the road that ran beside the country club. Some of the people were locals, attracted by the fame of the competitors or, more likely, by the news that something satisfactorily fatal had happened. The majority, however, were representatives of the media.

"Got a statement for us, Carol?" shouted one brash, overfamiliar reporter. When she shook her head, there was a general groan of disappointment. Staking out a closed site, and waiting for something—anything—to happen was boring in the extreme.

The car from the local station was taking longer than the promised five minutes, so Carol filled in the time chatting to the guard. His name was Steve and he'd been working for Gussie Whitlew for twenty years. "She's a great boss," he confided. "I did in my knee six months ago playing catch football with my kids, and she let me transfer from my guard job at the Whitlew headquarters, where I had to do a lot of walking, here to the country club."

"How strict is security here at the main gate?" asked Carol, already knowing from Anne's report that it varied between casual and totally slack. Indeed, when she'd arrived earlier that morning, the barrier arm had been up and no one had asked who she was, or what business she had to be there.

Steve rubbed his jaw, reluctant to answer her question. At last he said, "Well, to be truthful, not all that tight, if you get my drift, at least not up until this morning, when they found that poor girl's body." He held up a clipboard. "Now Jim and I, we've been told to stop every vehicle, both ways, and log them in and out."

Carol gestured at the contingent camped outside. "I saw reporters in the parking area this morning."

"Yeah, and I had the devil's own job to clear them out of there. It was a bit like trying to herd cats." He grinned at Carol. "Some of them have been trying to sneak back in, but Jim's out patrolling and I'm standing guard here, so only the accredited media people are on the course."

A marked police car came zooming down the road and turned sharply into the entrance, skidding to a stop at the boom gate. "My lift," said Carol.

Steve chuckled. Leaning forward, he said to the driver, "Hey, Hughie, slow down. The Inspector wants to get where she's going in one piece." Turning to Carol he explained, "We're mates. Hughie's been doing security at night around the course."

Carol got into the front seat of the car, and Hughie, slightly red, backed out to the road with a great deal more circumspection. He had a light build and a boyish, fair-skinned face, and looked absurdly young to be a police officer. "Sorry, Inspector, I was running a bit late."

"Your name is?"

"Oh, sorry again. Hugh Haver, but everyone calls me Hughie."

"Well, Constable Haver, you've been picking up a bit of extra money, doing security," she observed.

Hughie wriggled his shoulders, looking at her sideways. "Well, yeah. Only for a few days while the tournament's on."

"Were you the only person on patrol?"

"Yes."

"Does Vernon Coop know about it?"

His sheepish expression told her that he hadn't advised his superior officer. Hughie cleared his throat. "He asked everyone this morning, but I didn't own up. I had to shuffle the roster at the station around so I'd be free, but I didn't ask permission to do that, so I thought I'd better keep quiet."

He stared ahead, biting his lower lip. Carol said, "Even though there's been a suspicious death on the course? Surely you expected to be interviewed."

He looked glum. "I didn't use my real name. It was for cash—under the table, you know."

"Indeed?"

Flustered, he said, "I would have owned up if there was anything at all to say, Inspector, honest. I drove the perimeter of the course every fifteen minutes or so, all night, and nothing happened."

"You didn't see a single vehicle or person for the entire time?"

Hearing her highly skeptical tone, Hughie reddened. "Well, of course I saw a few other vehicles—people driving home or down to the beach or..." He took one hand off the wheel to make a you-know-how-it-is gesture. "I mean, there's always *someone* around."

"One of those someones may have been a murderer."

He ventured a glance in her direction, then looked away. "Honest, Inspector, I really didn't see anything unusual."

Carol said, "By the time I leave your local station, I want a full, written account of everything you remember from the time you started your patrol last night until the time you got home. Every single detail, including when and where you took a leak. Have you got that straight?"

Hughie swallowed. "Yes, Inspector Ashton." During the rest of their short journey he didn't speak again.

* * *

"May I introduce Mr. Vincent Goss," said Coop with a sarcastic half-smile. "Mr. Goss is a resident of an illegal squatters' camp in our local nature reserve." He shoved his face close to the seated man. "And you don't like to work, do you Vinny? Think the state owes you a living, eh?"

Carol calculated that, standing, Goss would tower over Coop. Goss seemed to Carol to be in his late forties. An angular man, his unkempt brown hair streaked with gray, unshaven, and dressed in reasonably clean but very worn, brown trousers and an equally ancient long-sleeved blue shirt, he sat with his hands in his lap, eyes downcast, apparently oblivious to Coop's words.

Carol looked around the interview room. It was like countless others she'd been in, filled with the familiar miasma of cigarette smoke, sweaty bodies, and fear. Terry Roham, trying to look severe—and failing—stood with his hands clasped behind his back. He had a lanky body and fine, curly hair cut very short. He was the newest member of her team, anxious to make a mark, but so far his impetuosity and tendency to cut corners had not impressed Carol. Terry reminded her of an oversize puppy, full of enthusiasm for life but short on self-discipline.

Detective Coop, standing with feet splayed and hands in pockets, said, "There's any number of offenses I can charge you with, Vinny, if you don't start talking—resisting arrest, for one."

Carol said, "I'd like to speak to Mr. Goss alone."

Coop was clearly surprised, and not at all pleased, to be dismissed. "I've already questioned him. Got nothing out of him, although some of his mates said he was off on the country club grounds last night." He shifted his glance to Goss. "Vinny's not cooperating, but then, what you expect from a no-hoper like him?"

Carol pulled out the battered wooden chair on the opposite side of the stained wooden table and sat down. "Mr. Goss," she said, "I'm Detective Inspector Carol Ashton. I'd like to ask you a few questions about a case I'm investigating." She glanced at the two men, signaling that she expected them to leave.

Terry Roham opened the door, his disappointment at being excluded obvious. Coop paused, irresolute. "You may not be safe in here alone," he said. "This bloke could be the one that did it."

"I'll scream for help, if necessary."

Her mocking tone narrowed Coop's eyes. "Suit yourself," he said, then followed Terry Roham out of the room, slamming the door behind him.

Goss raised his head. "The detective would be pleased if you did have to scream for help," he said in a deep and cultured voice.

Carol smiled. "I don't scream," she said. "It doesn't go with my position."

He made an amused sound, then said, "You can call me Vinny, if you like. I haven't been Vincent Goss for a long, long time." He raised one hand to knock his knuckles gently against the side of his head. "Scrambled," he said. "Before I had problems, I was a university lecturer. Economics. Isn't that a laugh?"

He slowly put his hand back into his lap. "I didn't resist arrest," he said. "I never do. Gives the cops an excuse to clobber you."

Carol said, "Have you heard what happened on the golf course during the night?"

Vinny tilted his head. "Bad news travels fast. Someone was killed on the headland. That's right, isn't it?"

"Yes, a young woman. Do you know anything that can help my investigation?"

He put his hands on the desk. Carol noticed that his nails were bitten to the quick. He saw her looking and said, "I've got a load of bad habits. I bite my nails and I drink too much and I smoke too much." He looked at her hopefully. "You wouldn't have a fag, would you?"

"I don't smoke."

"Too bad. I could use one." Vinny tapped the table, apparently deciding whether or not to confide in Carol. Finally he said, "There are kids, local kids, who harass us. They think it's fun to break things in our camp, rough us up a bit. Nothing too bad—just enough to make them feel like big men."

"Yesterday, you saw some of these kids?"

He nodded slowly. "Two of them in particular often come in the early evening to scout for lost golf balls to sell. I do the same thing, to get a little extra. I sell them at the driving range. For peanuts, of course, but better than nothing."

"And yesterday?"

"Yes. The two of them were there. I only know their first names. The taller, meaner one is Justin. He's a nasty bit of work. The other, younger boy is Ken. He's a follower, the sort that goes along with whatever someone stronger suggests."

Carol's opinion of the country club security sank a few notches further. "I believe, because of the tournament, there were extra efforts to protect the course from intruders," she said.

"If so, I didn't see it, and the boys weren't stopped." He smiled at her slyly. "The whole place is fenced, but that doesn't mean a thing. Getting under's easier than getting over. More than one place where there's a bit of cover with bushes growing near the fence and you can wriggle under. And if you want to risk your neck, you can always come up by way of the cliffs."

Carol had looked over the precipitous drop at the headland and assumed that no one could climb the crumbling sandstone, but she realized with chagrin that she hadn't made sure that this was true. "How difficult is it to climb? Have you tried?"

"Me?" Vinny gave a sudden cackle of laughter. "Haven't the head for heights." He sobered. "Haven't the head for anything much."

Making a mental note to check the cliff face as an escape route, Carol said, "What happened on the golf course last night?"

He rubbed his jaw, the gray stubble making a rasping noise. "There's this particular clump of bushes—you often get lost balls there, and a stream nearby where the players just leave the balls that go in because they don't want to get their feet wet. It was bright moonlight and I was looking around when I heard the kids coming. Hid under a bush, because last time the little bastards beat me up."

He paused, shaking his head. "No reason to hit me, but it's fun to them."

"Bright moonlight?" said Carol. "I don't imagine you'd find many lost golf balls by the light of the moon."

Vinny bit his lip. Carol waited. Eventually he said, staring fixedly at the table, "Got a bit of money, this afternoon. Nice lady in the supermarket carpark. She dropped some things, see, and I picked them up. She gave me a few dollars, probably to get rid of me. Anyway, I bought a bottle of sherry." He looked up. "Dry sherry," he said, as if this were an important point.

"I don't like sweet sherry myself," said Carol. "Now, what's all this to do with being on the golf course?"

"In the camp, see, we share things." Vinny rubbed a hand over his face, clearly embarrassed. "I didn't want to share this time. I hid the sherry, and when I got a chance I collected it and sneaked onto the course to drink it."

Great, thought Carol, a possible witness who was almost certainly drunk. Aloud she said, "And the boys, Justin and Ken?"

"There to cause mischief, I'd say."

"What happened next?"

"We all heard something—me and the kids. I saw them stop and look around."

"What exactly did you hear?"

"Raised voices, but not close. You couldn't make out any distinct words. But you could tell someone was really going off their head. It was fierce, I can tell you."

"One person was yelling?"

"The other one said something too."

"The voices, could you tell if they were male or female?"

"Not sure. Just voices."

Carol leaned forward. "Vinny, what time was this?"

Vinny raised his skinny shoulders. "Sometime after dark—not very late, though. Way before midnight. I don't have a watch. Don't need one."

"Okay, can you tell me where these people having an argument were when you first heard them?"

"Sounded like they were over near the cliffs. Somewhere in that direction. And the kids, they thought so too. They whispered to each other, and then they went off." He shook his head violently. "No way did I wait to see anything else. I got out of there, fast. There were too many people around for me."

He reached over the table and tapped hard on the surface in front of her. "You should find the kids. Ask them. They were heading in the direction of those two people."

"Are you sure?"

"I'm sure." He leaned back, satisfied. "Maybe one of them did it," he said.

CHAPTER SIX

Hugh Haver drove Carol and Terry Roham back to the country club. He gave monosyllabic replies to Roham's attempts at conversation and handed Carol several stapled sheets of paper when she alighted in front of the clubhouse. "This is what you asked for," he said.

She folded the pages into a square and shoved them into the pocket of her jacket. "I'll get back to you if I need more detail. And I haven't told Coop. I'll leave that to you."

Hughie nodded morosely and drove off.

"What was that about?" Terry asked.

"The constable was doing a little security work on the side, patrolling the course last night. I asked him for a report."

Terry opened his mouth to comment, but before he could speak, Carol said, "Vernon Coop's working the local connections to find those teenagers Vincent Goss claims were on the course last night. I want you to question the outside staff here—anyone who might have run into two boys named Justin and Ken, maybe when they were trespassing. These kids could be witnesses to a murder, and I want them found, fast."

Returning to Gussie Whitlew's office, Carol found Gussie herself at the open floor-safe. "Just looking for some papers," she said. "I'll get out of your way in a moment."

With the thought that Gussie Whitlew looked as perfectly groomed as she had that morning at the fourth hole, Carol said, "I was wondering if Fiona Hawk had a rental car. Did she go back to the hotel to change before the reception?"

Gussie stood up, dusting her hands. "I don't believe so. It wasn't necessary, as I'd made it clear the event was very informal."

"How did she get from her hotel to the country club in the morning?"

Gussie patted her perfect hair. "Limousine," she said. "If Fiona wanted a lift, she just picked up the phone. I have several drivers waiting on standby twenty-four hours a day."

"Did she order a driver last night?"

"I don't believe so. It would be just as easy for her to get a lift with any of the other players who'd opted for a rental car for the duration of the tournament." She smiled at Carol. "Do you like luxury cars, Inspector?"

"Why do you ask?"

"It's just that fast cars are one of my passions. I have a red Ferrari and a yellow Porsche. You must let me take you out some time. Or, better still, perhaps you'd like to drive one. Make your vehicle selection, and it's yours—as long as you take me along for the ride." Her expression indicated that she expected Carol to accept her offer.

"Thank you, but I'm fully occupied with this investigation."

"Then afterward, when you've caught whoever did this." Her enthusiastic expression became somber. "It's horrible to think that maybe it's someone I know, someone I talk to every day, who's done this dreadful thing."

Impulsively, she put a hand on Carol's arm. "It could be one of those homeless people from the camp. They're drunk and dangerous half the time. Have you checked them out? I've made numerous complaints to the authorities, but no one ever does anything."

"They've been interviewed."

Dropping her hand, Gussie let out a long sigh. "I keep seeing Fiona's face as she lay there in the sand, her eyes half open. It was grotesque, horrible."

It seemed to Carol that at some level Gussie Whitlew might be gaining a macabre thrill from the death. To forestall further discussion on the topic, she said, "Are you expecting a demonstration here tomorrow?"

Carol's question was short on detail, but Gussie's response was immediate. "Oh, God, yes! The blasted ecology people, the ones who have taken upon themselves to hate golf courses in general and mine in particular. They sent out a press release to announce they're picketing the Challenge. Mad, the whole lot of them. Call themselves, would you believe, Eco-Crones for the Environment. Bunch of middle-class elderly women who should have better things to do with their time." She added, sardonically, "Golf, for instance, would be an excellent diversion."

"Unfortunately," said Carol, "my Aunt Sarah happens to be one of those crones."

"You're joking."

"Afraid not."

Frowning, Gussie said in emphatic tones, "Then make sure she doesn't put one foot on my property, or I'll have her and her radical friends arrested for trespass so fast their little gray heads will spin."

"I've never had any success instructing Aunt Sarah to do anything she didn't want to do."

Gussie glared at Carol. "Then you'll have a jailbird in the family. And wait until some nosy reporter digs up the fact that she's related to the famous Detective Inspector Carol Ashton. Then the excrement will really hit the fan!"

"I hope," said Carol mildly, "you won't be tempted to leak that particular bit of information."

"Well, I'm tempted, but no, the secret of your activist aunt is safe with me."

* * *

By late afternoon both Anne Newsome and Terry Roham had reported back to Carol. The sum of their inquiries wasn't particularly helpful, although Terry did say that Joe Gallagher, the head groundsman, had said that he'd chased off a group of teenage boys on several occasions and that he had the impression that they lived somewhere close to the course.

Carol dispatched Terry Roham to find out if the fourth hole could be accessed from the sea with the admonition, "And please don't break your neck, Terry. It's just too much paperwork." He grinned and bustled out of the office, leaving her to wonder if her half-joking warning would tone down his natural impetuosity.

Mark Bourke called with the news that Davy Vere did have a minor criminal record, having been charged three times with common assault, but only suffered one conviction, for which he received, as a first offender, a suspended sentence. "The word is that he's the enforcer for his employer, Gussie Whitlew, and she looks after him with the best legal representation available."

"Anything on Major Hawk or his daughter?"

Hawk had been arrested for drunk driving twice, once in Britain and once in Australia, this occasion being only a week ago, when Fiona had been playing a warmup golf tournament in Melbourne. Fiona Hawk had no arrests of any kind, but she had been in touch with the British police about a stalker.

"A stalker?" said Carol. "Any details?"

"No one was ever apprehended. I've asked for available reports and should get them tomorrow."

"Have we got a name?"

"Just a first name," said Bourke. "The guy called himself Byron."

"That could conceivably be his last name."

There was a pause, then Bourke sighed. "Okay, Carol," he said, "I can read your mind. You want to know if any characters with the last name Byron entered Australia, particularly from Britain, in the last few days."

"Soon we won't even need a telephone," said Carol, laughing.

* * *

The identity of the body was now public knowledge, and the expected barrage of media requests for interviews, statements, or even a simple photo op, had been fielded by Gussie Whitlew's formidable public relations department.

Carol had been instructed to make a short statement to the media for the evening news. "This story is international news," said the superintendent, "so make it good, Carol. You know the drill."

The second day of the Whitlew Challenge finished with Toni Karstares leading, followed closely by Susann Johansson, nicknamed the Swedish Sensation, and then Ashleigh Piddock, who'd had a wonderful round with six birdies and one eagle. Completing the top five were Brinella Altunga and a Japanese amateur recently turned professional named Beth Shima. As Gussie had predicted, Kasha London had begun to fade, and had fallen to equal tenth.

Carol sent Anne to locate Toni Karstares, and also to request that Kasha London and Brinella Altunga not leave the clubhouse until they were interviewed. "And if Ralph Syncomm is anywhere around, I want to see him, too," she said.

Anne returned with a tall, confident woman striding behind her. "Toni Karstares," the woman said, leaning over the desk to shake Carol's hand firmly. "Let's get this over with."

When Carol introduced herself, Toni Karstares said, "I know all about you, Inspector Ashton. Gussie gave you a rave review."

She had a solid build, not fat but substantial, and broad shoulders. Her face was tanned and her short brown-blond hair was bleached by the sun. Carol noticed that her eyes were a startling cornflower blue. Her hands were graceful and long fingered. She was dressed for competition in navy blue shorts and a pale blue polo shirt with a sponsor's logo on the left breast and on the left sleeve.

Carol gestured for her to sit. Not mincing words, Toni said, "Fiona's dead."

"I'm afraid so."

"Accident or deliberate?"

When Carol made a no-comment gesture, Toni went on, "It's no secret I didn't like her. And she didn't care for me at all."

"Any particular reason why?"

Carol's question generated a scornful laugh. "I'd say so. Fiona Hawk was racist, virulently homophobic, and basically against anyone who didn't think she was the best thing since sliced bread. I lost out on two counts: I'm a lesbian, and I thought sliced bread beat her hands down."

Toni Karstares sat back and put one foot up on her knee in a relaxed pose. It was, Carol thought, an act to give an impression of ease, as there was tension in the woman's shoulders and a tic in her left cheek.

Toni said lightly, with no sign of strain in her voice, "You've no idea how delightful it is to speak about Fiona in the past tense."

"You argued with her yesterday before the day's play."

Toni, seemingly unfazed by Carol's statement, said, "So who didn't? She snapped at a couple of people, including me, then in the afternoon had a screaming match with her agent."

"I gather Ralph Syncomm and his company, SGL Agenting, represent several of the women golfers."

"Ralph's been trying to build up the list, although SGL is a small fish compared to IMG or some of the others. Ralph started representing me just after my career took off with a win on the LPGA tour three years ago, but once I was getting good media coverage, and had picked up a couple of excellent sponsors, he told me to stop being so outspoken. What he meant was, shut up about being gay. I wouldn't, he insisted, we parted ways."

"This screaming match between Fiona and her agent, what was it about?"

"I only came in near the end, so you should ask Ashleigh. She was a fascinated bystander because Ralph has just become *her* agent, and when someone like Fiona Hawk's accusing him of cheating to the tune of a million dollars or so, Ashleigh's attention was really caught."

"I presume you mean Ashleigh Piddock. She played well today."

"Yeah, the teenage sensation. The Venus Williams of golf. She's a bit of a brat, but basically okay."

Recalling that Uta Dahlberg had claimed that *she* was the agent for Ashleigh Piddock, Carol mentally added the young golfer to her list of interviews to be accomplished as soon as possible.

Carol said, "When was the last time you saw Fiona Hawk?"

"That would be in the rest room, some time during the reception last night. Maybe about seven. Fiona was parked in front of the mirror checking her make-up and, as usual she was bitching about something or someone, but don't ask me any details. I made it a rule to tune out anything Fiona said."

When Carol asked to whom Fiona was speaking, Toni Karstares laughed. "To anyone who'd listen, but specifically, in this case, to Kasha London. Kasha's a pushover for a sad story—she's too sweet for her own good. Frankly, she's just about the only one left on the tour who would pay any attention to Fiona's complaints."

"So Fiona Hawk was difficult?"

"*Impossible* to us—*charm* itself to the outside world. Like I said, a genuine, gold-plated bitch." She checked her watch, then stood. "Sorry, I've got to go."

Carol got up too. "This is just a preliminary interview. We will need to see you again."

Toni halted at the door, grinning. "I'm not going anywhere, Inspector Ashton—at least not until I win this tournament."

A couple of minutes later, there was a soft tap at the door. "Inspector Ashton, can I speak with you for a mo?"

Carol looked up to see the attendant who had shown her through the locker room facilities during Carol's tour of the clubhouse. "Ruth, isn't it? Come in."

"Ruth Gallant." She seemed considerably more subdued than when Carol had seen her a few hours earlier. "I wonder if I could have a word about what I said to you before?"

Intrigued, Carol gestured for her to sit down. "What would you like to say?"

"I've been thinking...I shot my mouth off a bit about Davy Vere and Fiona Hawk." Ruth gave an embarrassed smile. "Sort of exaggerated."

"Has someone been speaking to you about this?"

Ruth shook her head. "No, of course not."

"I believe you said that Davy Vere propositioned Fiona and that she laughed at him."

Ruth moved uncomfortably. "I made it out more than it was. He was just joking. It was nothing serious."

Carol sat back and considered the woman in front of her. The long silence clearly made Ruth nervous. "I'd better go," she said.

Leaning forward, Carol took a chance, saying in a stern voice, "Davy Vere told you to come here and explain you'd exaggerated."

Ruth flushed. "I told him I'd set it right." She licked her lips. "And I have."

"How did he know what you had told me?"

"Ah jeez—it was one of the other attendants." Ruth wriggled her shoulders. "This is a good job, you know. I wouldn't want to lose it."

"What exactly did Mr. Vere say to you?

Ruth groaned. "If you make me tell you, I'll get fired for sure."

"I don't think so."

"Okay," she sighed. "He took me aside and said he'd heard about what I'd told you and that I could kiss good-bye to my job if I didn't fix it up so you thought what I said before was a lie."

Ruth's face hardened, and some of the positive woman whom Carol had seen previously came to the fore. "Davy really is a bit of a bastard," she said. "He knows I'm a single parent and I can't afford to be out of work, even for a short time."

"What you first told me was true?"

She nodded reluctantly. "Yeah."

Carol said a few reassuring words and sent Ruth on her way. Then she sat, musing. Gussie Whitlew might have a high opinion of Davy Vere's talents—enough to forgive his surly nature. But surely even Gussie would blink if she knew he'd been threatening a member of her staff with dismissal if she didn't tell the story he dictated.

Carol found she was very much looking forward to interrogating Davy Vere.

CHAPTER SEVEN

Ralph Syncomm had told Anne he had an urgent appointment elsewhere so would like to see the inspector immediately. Ten minutes later he swept into the office, clearly intending to take charge.

"Inspector Ashton!" He pumped her hand hard. "I really am in quite a hurry, but I've made a little time for you."

She thought that he had made the best of a hollow-chested body and sharp facial features. His brownish hair was cut artfully to disguise, as far as possible, his incipient baldness, and his suit was beautifully tailored to minimize his weedy physique. He wore a heavy gold signet ring on his left hand, and an onyx ring on the little finger of his right hand. His watch, she observed without surprise, was a Rolex.

"Syncomm's an unusual name," she observed.

He flung himself down in the chair facing the desk and sat back, knees wide. "Yeah, it is an unusual name, but that's deliberate. Made it up, myself. You remember it, don't you?

It's all done legally. I was a Smith. Okay, you see the problem? Who'd remember Smith, and who'd forget Syncomm?"

"Ingenious," said Carol.

Syncomm frowned suspiciously, obviously wondering if this was sarcasm. Carol smiled at him pleasantly. "Could you tell me about golf sponsorships?"

He waved a manicured forefinger at her in a pay-attention mode. Carol thought that without much effort she could really learn to dislike Ralph Syncomm.

"Okay," he said, "basically the corporate sponsorship stuff is where the real dollars are. Professional golfers are walking billboards, and although the real money's with male golfers, the girls can rake in a fair amount too."

Carol thought he was the kind of person who would, if encouraged, talk himself into trouble. She said, "Would you mind explaining sponsorships a little more?"

Ralph Syncomm smiled expansively. "Not at all." Carol could almost hear him add the disparaging "little lady" to this sentence.

When she gave him an encouraging look, he went on. "Well, let's take your top lady golfer, eh? Okay, she's wearing a sun visor or cap, right? The center of the front is tops, but if I can get her to wear a cap, there's also the side panels and the back. There's a hundred thou, American dollars, right away."

"That much?" said Carol politely, when he paused for her reaction.

"Just the beginning. Anywhere the camera can pick up the client's logo or name is worth money. And that means the left sleeve is valuable, because that's the side on TV when she's putting. Okay? Then the left breast area…"

He paused to smirk. Carol waited patiently.

"Well, you see," he continued, "that position's really valuable real estate when she's a righty, because—you guessed it—the camera picks it up during play." He waved his hand in a circular motion. "There's other things—the golf bag, for instance, but the clothing's where the big bucks are."

"You take a cut of your client's sponsorship earnings?"

Syncomm seemed affronted, as though there was a hidden criticism in her question. "Yeah, of course. I do all the work, finding the sponsors, persuading them my girl's the one who'll give them the best bang for their buck, and then I have to set the whole thing up."

Syncomm paused to frown importantly at Carol. "The amount varies from company to company, and I have confidentiality agreements, in case you're going to ask firm figures." He added with a smug smile, "I can't reveal any of my negotiations—trade secrets, you might say."

Carol fiddled with her pen. "Apart from sponsorships," she said, "no doubt a player would be giving you a set percentage of her earnings."

He looked at her warily. "Yeah...?"

"I've heard a figure of twenty percent."

"Maybe you have." He examined his fingernails. "Sorry, I can't confirm or deny. In the ballpark, though."

"So if Fiona Hawk, who's at the top of the money earners, severs her connection with you and your company, that means you lose a considerable sum."

Syncomm grunted scornfully. "Now, Inspector Ashton, let's get this straight, eh? Fiona made me a lot of money; I'm not denying that. But there's plenty more up-and-coming young golfers who've got the potential to make the bucks."

"Fiona Hawk was threatening to sue you."

"Oh, please!" His long nose seemed to Carol to twitch with annoyance, making him appear, she thought, rather like an irritated rodent. "Trust me, it wasn't serious. Things got a bit heated, that's all. I blame Willoughby Hawk. He got her all stirred up over some accountant's error."

"You had a violent argument with Ms. Hawk in the corridor outside the locker rooms."

"Who said it was violent?"

"At least two witnesses."

Syncomm was thoroughly disgusted. "Karstares was one, wasn't she? Bloody dyke, causing trouble." He leaned his elbows on his spread knees. "Look, Inspector Ashton, these are top sports girls, and they're temperamental, just like any other entertainment stars." Shaking his head ruefully, he added, "And I have to tell you, Fiona was more temperamental than most. She flew off the handle at the slightest thing."

"I've been told she accused you of swindling her to the tune of a million dollars."

"There you have it! Typical exaggeration. The sum in dispute was only a few hundred thousand. And if you've heard there's any kind of legal action pending, that's wrong. Dead wrong."

Abandoning this line of questioning, she asked him when he had last seen Fiona Hawk.

"To speak to? When we had that discussion outside the locker room. I saw her at the reception, chatting up the right people, being photographed—all that stuff. I'd decided to let her cool down, so I kept away from her. Didn't notice her leaving."

"When did you leave the reception?"

Syncomm leaned back, arms folded. "I've no idea."

"Did you leave with somebody else?"

Carol's interrogation was clearly annoying him. "Are you accusing me of something?" he demanded. "You can't think I had anything to do with what happened to Fiona."

"These are routine questions."

Syncomm's thin mouth twisted into a bitter line. "Why are you persecuting *me*? If you want a suspect, try looking at Uta Dahlberg. She's been on the prowl to add to her stable of mediocre talent, and she approached Fiona when she heard we'd had a bit of a falling-out. Fiona told me she laughed in her face, saying she wouldn't dream of joining a second-rate outfit. And Uta said she'd get even."

* * *

Ashleigh Piddock drifted into the office, chewing gum and looking about fourteen, although Carol knew she was almost twenty. She was slender, pretty, had masses of springy, chestnut hair, and moved with the assurance of one who had her world under control.

She looked around with interest, then slumped inelegantly into the chair Anne indicated.

Carol, arms crossed, was half sitting on the substantial bulk of the floor safe. She'd decided to play the role of observer and let Anne lead the interrogation, as she was closer to Ashleigh Piddock in age, and probably in interests.

Anne started with, "Of course you've heard about Fiona Hawk's death and—"

"Omigod, yes! Can't believe it."

Anne waited, but apparently Ashleigh didn't intend to add anything more. Anne went on. "Yesterday you witnessed a heated conversation between Fiona Hawk and her agent, Ralph Syncomm. Is that right?"

Ashleigh shifted her gum from one side of her mouth to the other. "Sure. Just outside the locker room."

"You overheard what they were saying?"

"Like, duh!" said Ashleigh. "They were yelling, so who couldn't hear?"

"Who witnessed this, apart from you?"

Ashleigh gestured vaguely. "Like, everyone. Lots of people around, but Fiona didn't care. She's like, you screwed me over for the last time, you asshole."

"She was angry?"

Ashleigh gave Anne a pitying look. "That's what I'm saying. She's like, you asshole, and he goes, now calm down, Fiona. And she's like, get lost."

Carol smiled to herself as Anne plowed through a series of questions about the content of the disagreement. It soon was evident that Ashleigh either hadn't paid much attention or she wasn't willing to admit to specifics.

It was the same when Anne asked her when she had last seen Fiona Hawk.

"I was at the party thing, but if she was there, I don't remember seeing her. I left early, anyhow. It was boring." She stretched elaborately. "Now can I go?"

"One more thing," said Anne. "Have you recently changed agents?"

"I'm still with Uta," Ashleigh said, her face closing. "Why?"

"You're not switching to Mr. Syncomm?"

Ashleigh unwound herself from the chair. "Maybe. Anything's possible."

"Sorry," said Anne once Ashleigh had left. "I could have handled that better."

Carol smiled at her. "I don't think I would have achieved any more. That young woman is either totally self-centered or she doesn't want to tell us whatever it is she knows."

She broke off as a dark-faced young man, whom Carol immediately recognized as Eddie Altunga, came stalking into the office. "Which one of you is Ashton?"

Anne said coldly, "This is Detective Inspector Ashton, but who are you?"

Clearly dismissing Anne as unimportant, he turned his attention to Carol. "I'm Eddie Altunga, Brinella's brother."

Carol surprised him by putting out her hand, and saying, "Mr. Altunga."

He hesitated, then, obviously uncomfortable, shook her hand. Releasing her fingers, he said, "Why do you want to see my sister? She doesn't know anything."

Carol gestured him to a chair, but he shook his head. "I'm not here for long. So? What about Brinella? You shouldn't bother her in the middle of a tournament."

"Fiona Hawk was found dead on the course this morning."

"I know that," he said impatiently. "But it's nothing to do with my sister. Got that? She's not going to talk to you."

As he turned to go, Carol said quietly, "Mr. Altunga, not only will Brinella talk to me, you will too. Sit down. I have some questions for you."

"And if I don't?"

She didn't answer, but held his glance steadily. After a moment he looked away. Taking two strides across the office, he flung himself into the chair she had indicated previously. Arms crossed, he snarled, "Bloody cops. You're all alike where my people are concerned."

Although she kept her expression neutral, Carol felt a pulse of sympathy for the young Aborigine. She'd recently read a report that spelled out a picture of rage, despair, and violence for black Australia. With a rate of imprisonment fifteen times that of other citizens, Aboriginal people were eight times more likely to be murdered, and a staggering forty-five times more likely to be victims of domestic violence. And Australia's brutal history of intolerance and worse toward the country's indigenous people had left wounds that had been carried down from generation to generation.

"This appears to be a case of murder," she said, "so you understand I must question everyone who has had anything to do with the victim in the last few days."

Eddie Altunga grunted. Taking this as a positive sign, Carol nodded to Anne, who opened her notebook. The action made Eddie suspicious. "What are you writing down? I'm not signing anything."

"This is a preliminary interview. There may not be any need for you to make a formal statement."

Sinking his chin into his chest, Eddie said, "Yeah? Well, get on with it, will you?"

"How did you get on with Fiona Hawk?"

He rolled his eyes toward the ceiling with a stupid-question expression.

"Mr. Altunga?"

"She was a racist bitch. End of story."

Watching him closely, Carol said, "There was some sort of altercation between her and Brinella on Thursday morning."

He jerked upright. "Brinella told me what the bloody cow was suggesting, if that's what you mean." He shoved his chin out pugnaciously. "And I called her on it."

"You confronted Fiona Hawk?"

"At the reception on Thursday night. Got her in a corner and told her exactly what I thought of her."

"Did anyone witness this?"

Eddie's mouth twisted in half-smile. "You think I'd make a fool of myself, and embarrass Brinella, by yelling at the top of my voice? I kept it quiet, but Fiona bloody Hawk knew exactly what would happen if she repeated what she'd said—I'd sue the bitch for slander, and see how she liked being dragged through the papers."

He maintained that this was the last time he had spoken to Fiona, and that he and his sister had left the reception together rather early and had gone back to their hotel. He was vague about the time. "I don't wear a watch," he said, showing his naked wrist.

Carol followed a few more routine questions with, "I would like to speak with your sister."

With an air of triumph, Eddie said, "Well, you can't. Soon as she finished the round, Brinella had a photo op with a magazine. She'll be gone by now." He added with some satisfaction, "So you missed her."

"I'll interview her before the tournament begins tomorrow morning."

He bounced to his feet. "I won't have Brinella upset before she plays."

When Carol didn't respond, he snapped, "Typical. Bloody cops."

Gussie passed him as he barged out of the office. "Dear, dear, Inspector," she chided, "you seem to have upset Eddie."

"Not so hard to do."

"Not hard at all. That young man has a very short fuse. Now on another matter, Kasha's come down with a migraine. I've sent her back to her hotel, so you won't be able to interview her until tomorrow." She gave Carol a fetching smile. "I hope this doesn't ruin your interrogation schedule, Inspector."

Not waiting for a reply, she went on, "Did you have lunch?" Gussie's question was clearly directed only to Carol.

"I didn't have time."

Gussie clicked her tongue. "I insist you come with me immediately, and have at least something to eat." She directed a smile at Anne. "I'm sure Constable Newsome will hold the fort."

More interested in what Gussie Whitlew might have to say than in food, Carol readily agreed. Gussie took her to a small private dining room, decorated rather disconcertingly in regency style. Looking at the elegant furniture and delicate striped wallpaper, Carol said, "How charming."

Gussie laughed. "Astonishing, isn't it, in the middle of an ultramodern building?" She looked pleased with herself. "I like surprising people." Waving over a waiter who'd been standing attentively by the door, she continued, "Now what would you like?"

"Coffee would be nice."

"You can't live on coffee." Gussie was severe. "How about a glass of wine?"

"I'd prefer coffee—black, please."

"What am I thinking!" exclaimed Gussie playfully. "I've certainly seen enough police dramas to know it's quite unacceptable to offer alcohol when an officer is on duty." She paused. "Later, perhaps?"

"Thank you, but I don't think so."

"I'll see what I can do to change your mind. Now, allow me to order for you."

After a swift consultation, she sent the woman off with an order for two Caesar salads with grilled chicken, and turned back to Carol. "Today has been very difficult."

"I watched a little of the golf on the monitor in your room. It seemed to be going well."

Gussie's sunny mood abruptly disappeared. "As well as can be expected without Fiona Hawk," she said, her expression bleak. "Unless you follow golf closely, you can have no real idea of what a draw she was. A real personality. The sponsors loved her, she played the game skillfully and with real emotion, so the media loved her, and, of course, the fans loved her."

"Ironic, isn't it," said Carol, "that apparently to really know her was not to love her at all."

This got a reluctant smile from Gussie, who then observed, "Liam might give you an argument about that. He and Fiona were an item for some time."

Mentally searching the preliminary list of those close to Fiona Hawk, Carol said, "Her caddie, you mean?"

"You do impress me with your attention to detail," said Gussie with a raised eyebrow. "And yes, I'm talking about Liam Ivanovich. Quite a name for an Irishman, don't you think? His mother fell in love with a Russian, married the man, and carried him off to Dublin."

"I was under the impression that Ivanovich had been replaced as her caddie, and that he'd gone back to Ireland." Carol's tone was neutral, but she was irritated that Anne had failed to check this information.

"Their parting—remarkably for Fiona—was entirely amicable," said Gussie with a wry smile. "Liam's widowed mother had suddenly died, and he was returning to manage the family business—some tourist thing, I believe."

"Not very convenient, to lose your caddie on the eve of a big tournament, is it?"

Gussie pursed her lips, thoughtful. "I hadn't thought that through, but you're right. Liam would be very hard to replace. I know Fiona relied on his advice because he's one of the best at reading a course, so I'm surprised she didn't make more of a fuss when he said he had to leave."

"Who did replace him for the first day's play?"

"I'm not sure. Davy will know."

Anything unusual was worth following up immediately. Carol said, "Do you have an address or contact number for Ivanovich in Ireland?"

"He hasn't left Australia, although the plan was that he'd be flying home yesterday, so I was quite astonished to see him caddying for Kasha London when play started this morning. Right now, he's still out on the course."

Carol straightened. "I'd like to speak to him as soon as he comes into the clubhouse."

"Relax, Liam is no murder suspect."

Looking around, Carol saw a dainty antique desk with two modern handsets looking rather out of place on its polished surface. "I presume I can get through to your office on one of those phones?"

"Press the very top button," said Gussie. "As boss, I naturally take precedence."

Having set Anne on the trail of Liam Ivanovich, Carol came back to the table to find Gussie again sunk in gloom. "Without Fiona playing, the TV ratings won't be as good," she complained, "and you live and die by the ratings."

"Look at the media attention you've had today."

"It is true," Gussie conceded, "that in death Fiona has given the Whitlow Challenge more free publicity than we could ever hope for, but it's not good publicity."

"I recall you saying earlier today that your credo was that any publicity was good publicity."

Gussie had the grace to look a little embarrassed. "Did I say that? How gauche!"

She gave Carol a mock-appalled look. "Now, now, Inspector! You're not thinking I had Fiona murdered to gain international publicity for the tournament, are you?"

Carol raised her eyebrows. "Would you be capable of such a thing?"

"Oh," said Gussie, "I'm capable of anything."

CHAPTER EIGHT

The police divers reported to Carol after they had finished searching the water hazards on the course. Nothing of interest had been found, apart from many golf balls, two golfing gloves, and three clubs, one of them snapped in half. As a precaution, the clubs were being sent for forensic examination, but it was likely they had been flung into the water by highly frustrated players. "Found a whole bag of clubs last time I did a water hazard on a golf course," said one of the divers with a grin. "Now that was a *really* pissed-off player, willing to throw away that much money."

Then Terry Roham, jigging with enthusiasm, detailed the rigors of clambering around the rocks from the nearest beach and climbing the cliff face to the fourth hole. "If I hadn't found a local guy fishing on the rocks who pointed out the route, I wouldn't have thought there was a chance you could climb it."

"So you're saying any reasonably fit person could get up the cliff and reach the golf course?"

"Someone who knew where to start, and had a head for heights."

"How about going down from the top?"

Terry looked pleased with himself. "Yeah, I thought of that, so once I'd climbed up, I turned around and tried it. It's scary—the rock's pretty rotten, and you could come a real cropper, trying it—but it's possible."

"How about at night, in bright moonlight?"

Terry shook his head doubtfully. "I wouldn't even try, either up or down, but especially not down." He added cheerfully, "Maybe someone did give it a go, and fell off and got washed away in the tide."

"Interesting thought," said Carol, amused at his triumphant look of pleasure. "Check if any bodies have been washed up in this coastal area since last night."

Anne entered with Liam Ivanovich, whom she'd intercepted as he had come off the golf course carrying Kasha London's bag and clubs.

"Look, Inspector," he said as soon as he entered the room, "I've got to get back and clean and check all Kasha's stuff before I leave. And I've got people to meet, so will this take long?"

Assuring him that she would be as expeditious as possible, Carol assessed the man in front of her. He was wearing dark blue pants and overshirt with the player's name LONDON prominently displayed on his chest. Although of average height and build, he was quite strikingly handsome, with very black hair, very blue eyes, and very white skin. She wondered if such absolutes were also in his nature.

Recalling that Gussie had said that Ivanovich and Fiona had been, in Gussie's words, "an item for some time," Carol looked for some signs of sorrow or disturbance in his manner, but his expression showed only irritated forbearance.

True to her promise to be as brief as possible, Carol went straight to the point. "Fiona Hawk believed that you were leaving Australia yesterday to fly home because your mother had suddenly passed away. Because of this, she used a substitute caddie for the day's play. Was she aware that you had not left the country, Mr. Ivanovich?"

"No." He looked over at Anne Newsome, who had her notebook open. "Am I supposed to be making some kind of statement?"

"Not at this point, unless you wish to do so."

"Not at all." He had a slight Irish accent, which gave an attractive lilt to his speech. "Just tell me what you want to know. I've got nothing to hide."

It had been Carol's experience that those who announced they had nothing to hide almost always did. She said, "What caused your sudden change of plans?"

He made a face. "I decided not to go. Talked to my brothers and sisters, all six of them, and they had everything under control, so there was no point."

Thinking that if Ivanovich was grieving for his mother, he had it well hidden, Carol said, "When was this?"

"The day before yesterday. I'd already told Fiona I was leaving, so I left her thinking that I'd gone. I moved my stuff to a different hotel so I wouldn't run into her. It was easier that way."

Carol said agreeably, "Easier, how?"

Liam Ivanovich regarded her without speaking. Carol noticed that the shadow of his beard had turned the fine, pale skin of his lower face almost blue. Finally, he said, "Just easier."

"Did you arrange for someone to take your place as her caddie?"

"Didn't need to. Fiona said she'd handle it."

Carol probed a little more about his reasons for staying, and why he hadn't caddied for Fiona on the first day since he was available, but his answers continued to be terse and basically unhelpful.

"You caddied for Kasha London today. Why was that?"

Ivanovich spread his hands. "Why not? She was using some local guy, and I told her I'd step in, if she liked. She's a friend, so it was a favor, that's all."

"But," said Carol, "didn't you expect to run into Fiona Hawk? You've said it was easier to avoid her, but how could you do that when you were here at the club?"

"I'd heard Fiona had withdrawn," he said quickly.

"When did you hear this?"

Ivanovich scowled at her. "Are you trying to say that I already knew Fiona was dead? If you are, you're wrong. Ask Kasha. She called me at my hotel this morning not long before she had to tee off. I had to rush to make it here on time."

Deciding to speak with Kasha London before probing further into this interesting matter of how and when Ivanovich knew it was safe to come back to the country club because Fiona would not be there to see him, Carol changed the topic. "You and Fiona were close, isn't that so?"

"How do you mean?"

"You had a close, personal relationship."

He suddenly grinned, showing large, white teeth. Smiling, he paradoxically seemed much more formidable. "Are you asking if we were dating, Inspector?"

"Were you?"

"I had sex with Fiona—regularly. No strings."

"No strings on either side?"

"If you're asking if either of us cared much, the answer's no. I liked her well enough, and she felt the same about me."

"I've heard that Fiona had a reputation for being difficult to get on with."

"Not in bed, she wasn't," he said, with a short laugh. "She was into anything. A real athlete."

"Do you know anything about a stalker?"

He cocked his head. "The one in England? Byron, he called himself. More a pest than anything else, and typically, Fiona overreacted. He wrote to her, got her e-mail address—stuff like that. She never met him in person."

"She was worried enough to go to the police."

"I told you," he said, his scorn obvious, "she totally overreacted. It isn't as if she wasn't used to that sort of attention."

Carol's interrogative look encouraged him to expand. "Her fans," he said with an impatient snap in his voice. "The ones that want autographs are okay, but anyone as good looking as Fiona gets the weirdos who think she's going to fall in love with them."

"Does any one person come to mind?"

He shook his head. "I don't bother myself with them. Paying attention only encourages the losers, doesn't it?"

Another ten minutes' questioning got little more information, other than he had last seen the victim on Wednesday, the day before she died. Carol thanked him for his time, thinking as she did so that there must be more to his and Fiona's sudden parting of the ways than he was willing to reveal.

Carol crossed Ivanovich off her list of interviewees and ran through the other names. Davy Vere, added last, caught her attention. Carol realized that she was coldly angry about the way he had treated Ruth Gallant. She reminded herself that there were two sides to every story, but she still found herself saying with grim anticipation of the interview ahead, "Anne, would you find Davy Vere for me, please. I'd like to speak with him before the press conference."

While she waited, Carol called Vernon Coop at the local station, finding that he'd already gone home, but had left a message for her advising that there was still no luck in locating the two boys that Goss had claimed were on the golf course.

Anne came back with the news that Davy Vere wasn't available. "He's on his way to Melbourne," she announced. "It's urgent business—Gussie told me she'd sent him."

Noticing how easy it was to slip into a familiar, first-name basis when referring to Gussie Whitlew, Carol said, "Do you have any idea what sort of business?"

"She said it was something about sponsors. Nothing specific. And he'll be back tomorrow morning."

Checking her watch, Carol realized she wouldn't have had time for a long interview anyway. In deference to the necessity to have material for the evening television news, the media conference was to be held at five o'clock in one of the sumptuous clubhouse interview rooms.

Remembering Hughie Haver's report, which she'd put in her pocket and forgotten, Carol retrieved it and glanced at the three pages. He'd taken her instructions as gospel, so everything about his time patrolling the perimeter of the course was set out in exhaustive detail. She'd go through it later, at home.

She gathered her notes together, put them plus Haver's report in her briefcase, locked it, and put it out of sight under the desk, then walked with Anne to the assigned room.

There was a break in the buzz of conversation as Carol took the central seat behind the long oak desk on the raised platform at the front of the room. Once she was in place, the full bright lighting for the television cameras came on.

Squinting through the glare, Carol looked over the forest of microphones in front of her, recognizing many people, including Hilary O'Dell near the back. Carol beckoned to Anne. "Please tell Hilary O'Dell I'd like to speak with her after this ends. Then go home, Anne. Tomorrow's going to be a long day."

The murmur of conversations had risen in volume, and over the din a voice called out, "We've got a deadline here, Inspector."

"Perhaps we can begin," Carol said, her voice ringing out above the hubbub. Silence fell as all faces turned toward her. The strangers to Carol were almost certainly sports reporters who normally would not be attending a briefing on a murder investigation. She was sure that in another twenty-four hours journalists from Britain would join the throng. The Sydney Police Service PR Department had already been swamped with international calls, especially from the press in London.

After a brief statement identifying Fiona Hawk as the victim and giving deliberately vague details about exactly where her body had been found, and how she'd died, Carol fielded questions.

"So it's murder, is it, Inspector?"

"The postmortem has not yet been carried out, but I can confirm that we are treating this as a suspicious death."

A chorus of voices yelled for attention: "How'd she die?" "Any sexual attack?" "Got any firm suspects?"

One reporter, obviously with a contact in the neighborhood cops, said, "A homeless man's been arrested, hasn't he?"

"No one has been arrested. A local person has been helping us with our inquiries."

Helping with our inquiries was such a bland, essentially meaningless phrase, and Carol parroted it automatically, all the while thinking how Vernon Coop had protested when Carol had instructed that Vinny Goss be released after signing a formal statement.

Before she'd left the local station, Carol had had a quiet word with Vinny. "You must stay in the area, do you understand that?" He had nodded, and she'd gone on, "I'll need you to identify the two boys when we find them."

"Okay, but anyone at the camp could tell you if it was them. The little bastards have visited us often enough."

"I need you, Mr. Goss, because you were the one who saw the boys on the golf course last night. That's important."

He had sighed. "Okay, but I was trespassing, and Detective Coop says he'll nail me on that."

"Don't worry, I'll look after it. Are you planning to go back to the camp?"

His eyes had crinkled with amusement. "Where else would I go?" he had asked. "It's home, Inspector."

A woman in the front row broke into Carol's thoughts with, "Fiona Hawk was having major trouble with a fan—a stalker. Have you followed that up, Inspector?"

The reporter had a buzz-saw voice, much in contrast with her gamine face and slight body. She grinned, adding, "I'm sports, Inspector, that's why you don't know me. The name's Mandi Fiedler." She swiveled her head to take in the crush of media people behind her. "Mandi Fiedler, also known as the Melbourne Mouth. Isn't that right?"

There was general laughter, and someone called out, "Before they bury you, Fiedler, they'll have to beat your mouth to death with a stick."

"Oh, charming!" Mandi turned back to Carol. "Well, Inspector, got an answer on the stalker question?"

"I know it's a cliché," said Carol, "but I have to say it—we are following all possible leads."

"Oh, come on," called someone from the back. "You can give us more than that."

"Actually I can." There was a stir of interest. "A witness has reported that two teenage boys, probably locals, were on the golf course during the early part of last night, and may have seen or heard something of importance. The elder boy is called Justin and is about fifteen. The younger one is Ken, around fourteen. I must stress that we are sure of the names, but not of the ages. If anyone can provide information about these two boys—their full names, where they live—or if the boys themselves will come forward, we will be very grateful."

Carol reeled off the appropriate telephone numbers to call, adding that any police station would relay information if contacted, and then waited for the inevitable questions that would follow.

"Were these kids witness to the murder?"

"Are they suspects themselves?"

Carol said, "They are not suspects."

She gave a brief description of each boy. She'd decided not to bring in a police artist to work with Vinny Goss yet. The chances were that the boys, if locals, would be identified fairly quickly.

She finished with a final plea for anyone with any information to contact the police, knowing as she did so that, along with genuine calls, a small percentage of cranks would be dialing as soon as they saw the item on the news.

The crowded room emptied quickly. Hilary O'Dell was standing by with a wary expression on her face. Waiting until there was no one near them, Carol said to her, "I need a favor. I'm presuming you took photographs at the function here last night, and I'd like to see the proof sheets."

"That's a reasonable request. They're in my lab. I can bring them tomorrow, if you'll be here at the club."

"I'll be here in the morning, if that would suit you."

When the photographer nodded assent, Carol said warmly, "Thank you for your cooperation," knowing that Hilary O'Dell was well aware that the police could demand the proofs as possible evidence. "I'd like to go through them with you, and have you identify the subjects in the shots."

"Fiona will be in quite a few." Hilary gave a dry smile. "She was never backward in coming forward."

"Would it be possible to establish some sort of time frame?"

"The rolls are numbered in the sequence I took them, if that's any help."

"It should be." Carol smiled. "Thank you again, and forgive my rather terse treatment of you this morning."

As Carol turned away, Hilary O'Dell said, "Inspector Ashton, there is something else. I want to apologize."

"For what?"

"Those photos I took of you, when you got off the plane from America. I regret that, and I want to say I'm sorry."

Not trusting the veracity of this expression of regret, as after all Hilary O'Dell made her living catching newsworthy subjects off guard, Carol said, "Why are you apologizing now?"

She made an awkward gesture. "I suppose because I have the opportunity to, and I feel sorry about taking advantage of a bad situation."

Feeling a surge of anger similar to that when she'd opened the morning paper months before to discover her own face looking out at her, Carol said, "Water under the bridge. Forget it."

Of course, *she* hadn't forgotten. Being caught in the lens of a celebrity photographer, who then peddled the unflattering pictures to the press, had been more than unpleasant. It wasn't only that Carol looked like hell—she'd been exhausted, and recovering from injuries, including powder burns to her face— but the commissioner himself, his anger clear, had demanded to know why she hadn't taken steps to avoid this publicity. Implicit in the question was the suggestion that perhaps Carol had engineered the encounter with the photographer herself.

The whole subject of publicity as far as Carol was concerned had in the past months become a sore point with her superiors, especially as Carol had been encouraged to do an FBI course to let the media storm over an earlier, unfortunate case die down. Although it was hardly her fault that in the States she had become involved in a murder case—not as a police officer, but as a suspect—and that this had had the predictable effect of inflaming media attention even further.

"Here you are, Inspector!" Gussie, champagne glass in one hand, swept up to them. She still looked perfectly groomed, although Carol thought it must have been a long, hard day for her. "There's someone I want you to meet. Excuse us, Hilary, will you?"

She took Carol's arm and steered her out of the interview room and along the corridor outside. "I have a wonderful buffet available for anyone who needs a little sustenance. I'm sure you'll find something you like."

"And you're taking me to meet…?"

Gussie chuckled. "That was just a ploy. From the expression on your face I could tell you weren't enjoying your conversation with Hilary, so I rescued you."

"I assure you I rarely, if ever, need rescuing."

The buffet, Carol noted, was well attended by media representatives, including Mandi Fiedler, who waved companionably to Carol.

"What do you think of the decor?" asked Gussie.

It was a disturbing room, composed of oddly angled walls and dominated by a huge red mosaic that spread across part of the ceiling and dripped down one wall, rather, Carol thought, like a huge, squashed tomato.

"It has an impact," said Carol, opting for diplomacy.

Gussie laughed. "You hate it, I can tell." She indicated a chrome-and-red enamel bar. "Surely you're officially off duty now. How about some champagne? French, of course."

Carol's drink of choice was Scotch whiskey, but an excellent champagne was tempting. "Reluctantly, I think I'll pass."

Gussie took a sip from her champagne glass. "I believe you said you hadn't played much golf."

"I hacked my way around a few courses when I was much younger, but I wouldn't call myself a golfer, by any stretch of the imagination. A couple of times recently my son, David, talked me into playing a round with him, but he's so much better than I am that I'm afraid I provided more amusement than competition."

"You have a son?"

This wasn't a subject Carol intended to pursue in any detail. She said shortly, "He's a teenager. Lives with his father."

"We must do something about improving your game, Inspector, if only to impress your son. My pro here at the club is excellent. I'll arrange lessons."

"I'm afraid I don't have time."

"Not have time for golf? You might as well say you have no time for breathing!"

Carol was saved from making a response to this when her mobile phone rang. "Excuse me." It was Aunt Sarah.

"Darling, you know I hate to interrupt you when you're working, but I do need to see you tonight."

"Actually, I'm about to leave for home."

"Good," said Aunt Sarah. "I'll be there in an hour, and I'll bring pizza. Deal?"

"Deal."

"You're leaving?" Gussie seemed put out. She recovered to say, "Before you go, I have a request. As you know, I do hate formality, so I was hoping…"

"Yes?"

"I feel we're on such good terms, and I wondered…" She paused for a moment, then went on. "I wondered if I could call you Carol." She raised her eyebrows interrogatively, obviously fairly secure that Carol would agree.

Carol said pleasantly, "That would be unwise. I'm investigating a suspicious death. It's necessary to maintain a formal relationship with anyone associated with the victim."

Clearly surprised at this refusal, Gussie stared at her. Then a thin smile broke on her face. "Of course," she said. "I know what you're thinking. You have to bear in mind that there's a remote possibility that you might be arresting me."

She patted Carol's arm. "Later, when this is all over, I'm sure we can be friends."

CHAPTER NINE

"Darling, I thought I'd bring the pizza as a peace offering, and explain to you what's happening tomorrow. I don't want you embarrassed."

They were sitting, drinks in hand, on the wide deck at the back of Carol's house. Black-and-white Sinker sat on the railing and washed his whiskers—Aunt Sarah had brought him a gift of fresh fish, and he was meticulous about cleaning himself after this delicacy. A fitful breeze, filtered through eucalyptus gums, drifted up from the expansive waters of Middle Harbour far below. A rare black cockatoo, one of two Carol had recently sighted, flew overhead, shrieking a harsh farewell to the day.

Looking over at Aunt Sarah, Carol smiled affectionately. Her aunt had been a reassuring constant from childhood—warm, welcoming, and with a delightful flavor of eccentricity. She was short, chubby, and dauntingly energetic. Her deeply tanned skin was leathery from a lifetime of outdoor activities, and her hair, bleached white by sun and time, sprang in a halo around her head.

Smiling at her affectionately, Carol asked, "Just what are you planning to do at the country club? It doesn't involve public nakedness, does it?"

Aunt Sarah was not a stranger to protests—over the years she'd been arrested in demonstrations against the war in Vietnam, French testing of atomic weapons in the Pacific, rights for Aborigines, and the treatment of animals in laboratories. Lately she'd concentrated her efforts on environmental causes, particularly in the Blue Mountains where she lived. She was the guiding light in several local groups dedicated to protecting the beauties of the area from overdevelopment.

Head on one side, Aunt Sarah looked at her niece assessingly. "You know, Carol, you've been different since you came back from America. A little more relaxed, and definitely showing more of a sense of humor."

"I'm pleased you're pleased." Carol took a sip of her Dimple Haig, then gently swished the whiskey so that the ice tinkled against the glass. "It just so happens that I met someone in the States who was on her way to Australia on business."

Aunt Sarah slid to the edge of her chair. "Yes?"

"She's with the FBI—Leota Woolfe."

"Ah!" Aunt Sarah nodded sagely. "I see."

"I've mentioned her, I'm sure."

Her aunt grinned. "You have, but not in enough detail. Would you care to fill me in?"

"Not really, but I promise you if it's possible, I'll arrange for you to meet her, although she's only in Sydney for a couple of days. Most of the time she's going to be in Canberra liaising with the federal cops." Carol glanced at her watch. "Her flight's well underway by now."

Showing signs of the keenest interest, Aunt Sarah inquired, "Are you going to meet the plane?"

"I can't, even if she wanted me to—which she doesn't. Her flight gets in at six tomorrow morning, and I've got a seven o'clock appointment at the morgue."

"You're serious about this woman?"

"It's a friendship."

Her aunt frowned. "I can't see much future in a long-range relationship."

"Thank you for your input," said Carol, her tone dry. To forestall further questions, she changed the subject. "Let's get back to your scandalous activities. What is it that is going to embarrass me?"

"Inspector Carol Ashton shouldn't be associated with a rabble-rouser," said Aunt Sarah, clearly pleased with her self-description. "That's why I'm staying with Sybil."

Sybil's name hung between them. Carol wanted to say something, but wasn't quite sure what. Aunt Sarah removed the problem by speaking first. "I know you're about to say that you and Sybil are just friends. Did I take the words out of your mouth?"

"Can we drop this topic?"

"That's the terse Carol I used to know," said her aunt, not approvingly. "And yes, we can change the subject to golf courses and why they destroy the ecology."

"I feel a lecture coming on."

"Do you have any idea of the harmful impact these golf courses have on our quality of life? Not only do they take up valuable land that could be parks and reserves and playing fields for everyone—not merely for a select few—but they also poison the environment. The courses may look like lovely green areas to you, but they're killing zones!"

Resigned to hearing the details, Carol said, "They are?"

"I know that tone, Carol. You're not really listening, but you should! Fertilizers, insecticides, weedicides, everything-icides! The amount of chemicals poured onto a golf course to keep it green, to destroy all insects, weeds—anything natural that belongs there—is staggering. And the runoff!" Aunt Sarah gestured vigorously. "In the case of the Whitlew Country Club, not only do they defile the land, the runoff goes into the sea, too. God knows what it's doing to marine animals!"

"I suppose you have studies—"

"Of course we have studies! It must be brought to the general public's attention. And a demo at an international golf tournament is a perfect way to do that."

More temperately, Aunt Sarah added, "And we could get international coverage. *Most* important. Do you have any idea how many golf courses there are in Britain and the United States?"

"How many?" said Carol.

Aunt Sarah looked flummoxed for a moment. "How many? I'm not sure of the exact number, but it's a lot."

"Gussie Whitlew told me you were calling yourselves Eco-Crones."

Aunt Sarah, her green eyes, so like Carol's, narrowed dangerously, demanded, "Is it the *eco* or the *crone* you're objecting to? You're not ageist, are you, Carol? I'm sure the Whitlew woman has plenty to say about old women causing trouble."

Recalling Gussie's words about the demonstrators, Carol smiled reluctantly. "Yes, she did have some rather harsh comments. It's fair to say she thinks of your group as middle-class, gray-haired troublemakers."

"Good. That's just what we are. Forty women of mature years who have a mission to save our planet for future generations. We'll be a force to be reckoned with tomorrow."

With foreboding, as Carol knew her aunt was inexorable when energized by a worthy cause, she asked, "Just what are you planning to do?"

"We'll demonstrate. Wave placards. Chant. Oh, and we're doing a little street theater—that always gets attention from the media." Aunt Sarah beamed at her. "You haven't seen anything until you see me play a pesticide-contaminated butterfly."

Carol couldn't repress a chuckle at the vision this conjured up. Her aunt was not amused. "Laugh all you like, my dear, but it's our environment that's being irrevocably poisoned."

Still grinning, Carol said, "I can see I shouldn't miss this performance tomorrow."

"But you mustn't be there, Carol. When we're asked to move on, we intend to use civil disobedience. We will almost certainly be arrested. I fully intend to be dragged screaming into the paddy wagon."

"No one will know you're my aunt."

"But what if the media find out? A shot of Carol Ashton watching calmly as her close relative is summarily arrested— and believe me, I'm going to make a real fuss—wouldn't be very good publicity as far as your career is concerned, would it?"

"Probably not."

"Besides," said Aunt Sarah complacently, "with a bit of luck you'll be able to catch the whole thing on television tomorrow night."

* * *

Later that evening, after her aunt had hugged Carol and had rattled off in her battered station wagon, Carol called Mark Bourke and discussed the findings of the day.

"Forensic found traces of tissue and blood on the head of the sand wedge," said Bourke. "Same blood type as Fiona, so I'd say we have our murder weapon."

"I suppose it's too much to hope that the owner had her initials engraved on the shaft?" Carol said facetiously.

"No initials," said Bourke, "but did you know that pro golfers use forged-blade irons, each hammered out from a piece of metal? Ordinary, everyday players make do with cast-iron clubs, mass produced like sausages."

"Sausages?"

Bourke chuckled. "You know what I mean. And this is of interest, Carol, because the sand wedge used to beat in Fiona's head was the professional version, tailored specifically for a particular player. Brand name Dandon, which is the new Korean outfit trying to muscle in on the established sporting equipment manufacturers."

Visualizing the logos she'd half noticed during the day, Carol said, "Dandon uses a green spiral enclosed by a red square for its logo, doesn't it? I'm sure I saw it on the clothing of at least two of the players today, but I've no idea which ones."

"That's the logo, all right. The company doesn't have an office here, so I've got a call into Seoul, and also one into Dandon in the United States, but no answers yet. And I'll also try chasing up a sports agent or two tonight. By tomorrow I'll have the names of the sponsored players for you."

She told him about Aunt Sarah's intended activities and left him chuckling, as he was particularly amused by the name Eco-Crones.

Carol poured herself a nightcap and retrieved her briefcase, which she'd dropped by the front door. She unlocked it with difficulty and, puzzled, looked at the briefcase closely. It had a comparatively flimsy fastener, and this had been sprung with some tool, probably a screwdriver, then forcibly pushed together again so that it relocked.

She went through the contents quickly. The only thing missing was the report she had demanded from Coop's young officer, Hugh Haver—a report she hadn't yet had time to read.

Thoughtful, she took her drink and went to sit with Sinker in the velvet darkness of the summer night. Cicadas trilled, then fell silent. What was in the report that necessitated breaking into her briefcase? She'd left it under the desk when she'd gone to the media conference and picked it up before she'd left for home. First thing tomorrow she'd ask Hugh Haver for another copy.

Sinker, tail lashing, was riveted by the beguiling rustle of something moving in the garden and disappeared off the deck.

Carol wasn't concerned that he'd catch anything. Unlike Jeffrey, Sybil's imperious ginger cat, Sinker was the feline world's most inept hunter. When Carol and Sybil had been living together, Sinker would proudly stalk in with a dead mouse in his mouth, pretending that he had caught it, and not simply picked up the little corpse after Jeffrey had abandoned it.

Sybil. She could picture her so clearly, with her red hair, slim body, and implacable will. It would be a comfort, albeit a cold comfort, to acknowledge that this chapter of her life was concluded, but Carol was aware that nothing really had been resolved.

Her thoughts turned to Leota Woolfe. If Sybil was the past, was Leota the future? Carol shook her head, downed the last of her whiskey, and unfolded herself from the deep-seated redwood deck chair.

"Are you coming to bed?" she said to Sinker, who had reappeared without prey and was washing behind his ears with deep concentration.

The moon was rising over the treetops, turning everything to a black-and-white contrast. Carol looked up at its serene disk and imagined twenty-four hours before, when Fiona Hawk's dead face had been washed by its light.

Who had seen her still features silvered by the moon? Her murderer, of course. And perhaps Justin, the kid trespassing on the course. Tomorrow, if the two boys hadn't been located, she'd bring Vinny Goss in to work with a police artist.

"The problem," Carol said to Sinker, "is how she was persuaded to go up onto that headland. Do you have any ideas?"

Sinker yawned. Apparently he didn't.

CHAPTER TEN

"Such a pity, she's a fine-looking young woman," said the pathologist, Jeff Duke, surveying Fiona Hawk's naked body lying on the metal autopsy table.

"And it wouldn't be a pity, if she was less good looking?"

Duke laughed as he strapped on a full-length rubber apron. "Feeling a trifle acerbic this morning, Carol?"

Her paper gown rustled as she adjusted her paper mask. "Anyone's death diminishes me."

"Ah!" Duke was elated. "You're paraphrasing John Donne. 'No man is an island' is the title of that particular sermon, I believe." He snapped on latex gloves, continuing in oratorical style, "Ask not for whom the bell tolls. It tolls for thee."

Duke's assistant, a stout, balding man with protruding, pale blue eyes groaned theatrically. "Cripes," he said, "we're in for Jeff's full repertoire this morning. Just wait, Inspector—soon he'll be launching into his favorite bits of Shakespeare."

"To be, or not to be, that is the question," said Duke, swiftly making a Y-shaped incision that laid open the chest and abdomen.

Underneath her mask, Carol winced. She'd observed many postmortems but had never become inured to this final, necessary violation of a victim. Soon the body in which Fiona Hawk had felt and thought and moved would be catalogued: every part of her, her organs, her brain, measured, weighed, examined, and commented upon in dry, forensic language.

Duke and his assistant were working with swift efficiency. The thin whine of a bone saw put Carol's teeth on edge. This was the part of a postmortem she had always found particularly disturbing, where the body was neatly scalped, the skin sliding off the bone so that the dome of the skull could be removed and the naked brain exposed.

To distance herself from the official butchery taking place before her, Carol thought about the conversation she'd just had with Leota Woolfe, who had arrived in Sydney right on schedule at six o'clock. Carol had explained she was caught up in an investigation, but would make sure she had some time this evening, if Leota didn't think that she'd be too jet-lagged.

Leota had scoffed at the very concept of jet lag. "We FBI types are tough," she'd declared. "Anyway, I can always fall asleep in your arms."

"Carol," said Jeff Duke, jerking her attention back to the chilly, functional room where the pathologist was holding Fiona's brain in his gloved hands, "look at this. She sustained two blows to the head, not delivered at the same time."

"What are you saying?"

"See here? She was hit from behind, hard enough to cause a slight bone fracture and to bounce the brain against the skull and bruise the surface. This wasn't enough to kill her, but she'd almost certainly be, if not unconscious, very close to it."

"How long before the final, fatal blow?"

"Probably ten minutes, maybe less. Much more force was used this time, so the skull shattered, and fragments of bone were driven into the brain."

"A golf club was found with the body."

Carol knew Duke was smiling under his mask. "Indeed," he said, "a sand wedge, I believe. Myself, I'd use a driver. More speed at the club head."

* * *

It was still early when Carol got to the Whitlew Country Club, and she was relieved to see that Aunt Sarah and her Eco-Crones had not yet arrived, although a TV broadcast van was already parked near the entry gates. Steve was on guard duty, and she stopped at the boom gate to chat with him for a moment.

"Gussie tells me we've got a demo likely today," Steve said as he jotted down her name on a log. "We've brought in extra guards from head office to beef up the security."

"And the local police have been alerted?"

"Yeah, I did that yesterday. They'll send a patrol car if things look dicey, but it's only a bunch of greenies—old women, Gussie says—so there'll be no probs."

Thinking that obviously Steve had not run into anyone like her Aunt Sarah before, Carol said, "You know, of course, that citizens are entitled to demonstrate."

Steve looked rather affronted that Carol had thought it necessary to point this out. "Well, yeah. I know people's rights. I've seen my share of demos, and even marched a few times myself way back when I was a student. Don't give it another thought, Inspector. Just so long as they don't trespass or block the traffic, she'll be apples."

Parking her car, Carol thought that trespassing and blocking traffic were probably exactly what these particular demonstrators intended to do.

As Carol walked into the reception area of the Whitlew Country Club, Mandi Fiedler stopped her by the central fountain. "Inspector Ashton, I would like a private word with you, please."

Again Carol was struck by the contrast between the reporter's metallic, abrasive voice and her almost childlike form. Her dark hair was tousled, her face innocent of any makeup, her smile street-urchin roguish.

Mandi gestured at the chrome figure of the golfer forming the fountain's central structure. "Who do you think was the model for that?"

"I've no idea."

"Fiona Hawk."

Carol frowned up at the figure. The statue was very definitely female. Water cascading from the head of her upswung club showered over her face and shoulders, then splashed into the foaming surface of the surrounding pool. "It's so stylized it doesn't look like anyone in particular."

Mandi grinned at her. "It's at this point that I say those always intriguing words..." She paused, then went on in a dramatic whisper, "There's something you should know."

Carol, having no intention of playing along, said peremptorily, "Then tell me."

"Let's discuss it over coffee. I promise you that it won't be a waste of your time."

There was something about the reporter's manner that convinced Carol to agree. "You have fifteen minutes," she said.

The country club had an Art Deco tearoom dispensing a wide range of blends of both tea and coffee. Carol looked around with pleasure. She always liked Art Deco as a decorative style, finding the geometric forms quite delightful.

Mandi Fielder commandeered a corner table, ordered coffee and doughnuts and, after the waiter had gone, said to Carol, "Trade? It's only fair."

"If you want an exclusive, I'm not giving you one. Any statements I make will be to the media in general."

"You're a hard woman, Carol Ashton," Mandi said, not at all put out by Carol's response. "Even way down south in Melbourne we've heard all about you." She broke off as their coffee and a selection of doughnuts arrived.

Carol found herself hungry. She hadn't been able to face breakfast before the postmortem, and when she'd left Jeff Duke the smells and images she carried with her had canceled out any thought of food. She looked at a cream-filled doughnut warily, and instead tried a plainer cinnamon one.

Mandi took a huge bite from a fat chocolate specimen, screwing up her face with delight as she chewed. "I love this stuff," she said, "and I never put on any weight, however much I eat. Maddening, isn't it?"

"What exactly is it I should know?"

"We sports writers," said Mandi, obviously intending to take an oblique path rather than directly answer the question, "don't get a great deal of respect from the other so-called serious journalists. If you can't promise me a scoop, can I at least hope for some tidbits of background information? If you can do that, I'm willing to tell you what I know."

"Of course," said Carol, sure that someone like Mandi Fiedler wouldn't be satisfied with anything but the inside story. Carol fully expected that whatever Mandi said now, she would try and call in the favor in the future.

After demolishing a second doughnut, Mandi said, "Several of the women played in a golf tournament in Melbourne last week, sort of as a warmup to the Whitlew Challenge."

Carol looked at her watch. Mandi chuckled. "I can take a hint, Inspector, so I'll give you the pithy version. Okay, so I was covering the tournament, doing background stuff on the notable players, human interest stories, and so on. One afternoon after play had finished for the day, I found myself one-on-one with Fiona Hawk over drinks at the clubhouse bar. There she was, all by herself, chug-a-lugging Southern Comforts like they were going out of fashion."

"You did an interview with her?"

"Not exactly, it was more like a girls' heart-to-heart, if you see what I mean. Maybe Fiona was tired or maybe it was the bourbon or maybe she was just generally pissed off—whatever the reason, she was very forthcoming about Gussie Whitlew."

"In what way?"

After taking time to demolish yet another doughnut, Mandi wiped her fingers delicately on a napkin and continued in her rasping voice, "The only person I've told about this conversation with Fiona is my husband, and he's silent as the grave."

"I can't promise that."

"I don't expect you to—in fact, I'm telling you about this because it might have something to do with Fiona's death."

She gave Carol a level look, then went on, "Okay, so Fiona and I are getting to be best friends, and she confides that Gussie has been pursuing her for some time, begging Fiona to play in the upcoming Whitlew Challenge in Australia. She tells Fiona she's got some of the best in the world lined up, but Fiona is the shining star of the sport."

"I can't imagine why Fiona wouldn't want to be involved," Carol observed, "considering the prize money being offered."

"For whatever reason, Fiona played hard to get, so Gussie went to the trouble to attend matches where she was playing in both Europe and the States. In a final effort to convince her to agree, Gussie assured her that Fiona was the inspiration for the expensive decorative fountain that would greet everyone entering the country club."

"Flattering," said Carol, pouring herself another half cup of the excellent coffee.

"Very, but Fiona told me she hadn't been keen to accept, even though Ralph Syncomm, her agent, was all for it—his mouth was watering at the prospect of the million-and-a-half winner's purse."

Carol raised an eyebrow. "And this is where I finally learn the something I should know. Right?"

Mandi Fiedler threw back her head and laughed. "You're too perspicacious for me, Inspector. You already know, I imagine, that Gussie is picking up the tab for all the golf stars she's invited to play in her tournament. Apart from appearance money, she's covering airfares, hotels, rental cars, and so on. It helps she's richer than God."

"And in Fiona Hawk's case?"

"In Fiona Hawk's case there was rather more encouragement, such as bonuses if she made the top five each day of play, various expensive presents, and the promise of a Ferrari—a red one to match Gussie's. There were strings attached, of course. Put bluntly, Gussie had a sexual interest in Fiona, and expected her to at least acquiesce, if not downright welcome, Gussie's advances."

"And she didn't?"

Mandi made a face. "You know," she said, "I got the strongest feeling that Fiona had been playing Gussie for a fool right from the very start and had every intention of taking what she could get from her and no intention of ever providing what Gussie wanted."

Carol swallowed the last of her coffee, sent a regretful glance in the direction of the remaining doughnuts, and said, "Why are you telling me this now?"

"At the end of our conversation, Fiona had second thoughts about baring her soul, and swore me to secrecy. What with our Aussie libel laws, and both Fiona's and Gussie's hardball reputations, agreeing to keep quiet wasn't difficult. I put the whole thing into my interesting-but-of-no-use mental file—that is, until last night."

"Last night Davy Vere went to Melbourne."

Mandi Fiedler looked at Carol with genuine admiration. "You are a crash-hot detective, aren't you! That's absolutely right. I got the word that Davy Vere was asking questions, leaning on people, making threats—his usual way of playing Gussie Whitlew's enforcer." Anger suddenly washed over her face. "He even approached my husband."

Mandi leaned over the table to say in a confidential tone, "And do you know what's really interesting, Inspector? I hadn't said anything to anyone. I'm guessing Fiona told Gussie that I knew enough to spill the beans, and Davy was sent to Melbourne to find out if it was true." She settled back in her chair. "Worth following up, don't you think?"

"Definitely," said Carol.

* * *

Leaving the tearoom, Carol pulled out her mobile phone and called the local police station. When she got Hugh Haver on the line she asked him to bring a copy of his report over to the country club as soon as possible, apologizing that she'd mislaid the first one he'd provided.

As she neared the reception desk, she saw with pleasure that Mark Bourke was coming through the chrome entrance doors. He wasn't handsome or flashy or charismatic. Mark was substantial, in every sense of the word. She trusted him totally, respected his abilities, admired his calm, pleasant manner. He was her colleague, her friend, and something more. When they worked together on a case they struck sparks from each other. It was teamwork of the highest order, and Carol enjoyed the thrust and parry, the unexpected insights, the chase toward a conclusion that would bring a solution to a crime and a sense of justice served.

"Before I forget," he said when he reached her, "Anne's going to be late today. There's been a problem with her mother."

Carol led the way over to a nest of red leather lounge chairs. "Something serious?"

"You know she's got Alzheimer's, and she's pretty far gone. The poor old dear wandered out late yesterday and got herself lost. Anne was frantic, but some good citizen found her mum and took her into a hospital emergency room early this morning. She's got cuts and bruises, but seems to be okay. Anne's staying with her until her brother can get there and take over."

With a touch of shame, Carol realized that the fact that Anne's mother suffered from Alzheimer's disease had passed her by. Perhaps she'd been told this fact, but she certainly hadn't paid any attention at the time. In fact, when Carol thought about it, although Anne Newsome had worked with her for several years, apart from her professional side, Carol really knew very little about the young constable. Perhaps concern for her mother was the reason Anne had neglected to check that Liam Ivanovich had, in fact, left Australia.

Bourke handed her a manila envelope. "Photos of the bracelet found in the bunker. Forensic says no usable prints on it. It's expensive, and unusual, so somebody should recognize it. Since Anne isn't here, I'll take these around myself and see if someone's eyes light up with recognition."

Carol took out one of the photos and studied it. "Accidentally dropped, or planted?" she asked.

"I'm leaning toward planted. Of course, the bracelet could have been lost days ago by some innocent golfer trying to blast her ball out of the bunker."

"What about the golf club artistically arranged with the body?"

"With the aim to incriminate someone?" said Bourke. "If so, there are only three players using the Dandon brand—Brinella Altunga, Susann Johansson, and Heather Weller."

With a wry laugh, Carol said, "The list of potential suspects is growing longer by the moment."

"We'd better get a wriggle on, Carol. Two days' play, and then, after the tournament ends tomorrow, there'll be wholesale jetting out of the country of prospective witnesses and, who knows—maybe a murderer or two. And speaking of murder, how was the post this morning?"

Carol wrinkled her nose. "The usual. And Jeff Duke was in a good mood, which really adds to the experience."

Bourke laughed. "Was he into poetry? He quoted damn near all 'The Man from Snowy River' to me last time I was there."

"It was John Donne and Shakespeare today, but he took time off to give some preliminary results."

She ran through the findings: no sexual attack; one blow to the head to induce unconsciousness, then a little later a second blow, which caused death almost immediately; the wound to the right side of the head was consistent with a weapon similar to the golf club that had been found with the body; the final impact was most likely delivered when the victim was lying on her back; lividity indicated that the body hadn't been moved after the fatal blow; death had occurred some time between nine o'clock Thursday night and one o'clock Friday morning.

"A four-hour window makes it difficult," he said, shaking his head. "We seem to have any number of witnesses whose sense of time is slippery, to say the least."

Carol told him about the report missing from her briefcase. "There was no one around in the admin offices when I left for the media conference, so anyone could have walked in, forced the lock on my briefcase, and taken the report."

"There must be something interesting in it."

"Or somebody thought that there was. I glanced at it, and there were three tightly typed pages that would take some time to read carefully. I'm sure that's why Haver's report was removed. Obviously I can get another copy, so there's no point in destroying it."

"I'll give it the fine-tooth-comb treatment when Haver delivers the replacement," said Bourke, "but in the meantime let me give you a quick report on my investigative efforts. First, regarding Fiona's British stalker, there's no record of a Mr. Byron entering Australia, and the English cop I chatted with said that the general opinion was the man didn't exist—that Fiona Hawk had made him up, apparently just to get extra media attention. You know the stuff, *Sports Star Stalked* headlines."

"Ms. Hawk becomes more charming by the minute," Carol observed.

"Second, Uta Dahlberg's company is in financial trouble, and she urgently needs a big name client, or she's up the proverbial creek without the paddle."

Carol remembered Uta Dahlberg's incandescent intensity. With her black hair, white face, and burning eyes, she certainly looked dangerous, and perhaps she was.

"Third," said Bourke with an indulgent smile, "my Pat's coming to the Challenge today, having talked her mother into baby-sitting, and she wants to know if you can make time to have a quick coffee with her."

"Pat's keen on golf?"

Bourke gave her a world-weary look. "My beloved wife is keen on anything that involves hitting a ball or riding a horse. That makes polo her ideal sport, but she's recently discovered golf. She's even dragged me out on a course a few times, and the result wasn't pretty."

"Good heavens!" exclaimed Gussie Whitlew, sweeping up to them. "You can't possibly carry on confidential conversations out here in the reception area. My office is waiting for you, and I'll arrange refreshments immediately."

Today she wore an outfit consisting of floating panels of blue and green silk. Grinning, Bourke caught Carol's eye, and she remembered his disparaging description of Whitlew fashion items as *those colorful flappy things*.

"We'll be taking formal statements today," said Carol. "Ms. Whitlew, I'd like to make a time for you to be interviewed."

"Me?" She was plainly astonished. "I can't see why you need to have me make a statement. Of course I'm appalled and upset by what's happened, but I personally know nothing of any help to you."

"We need information on the Whitlew Challenge," said Carol smoothly. "How it's set up and run, who's involved, that type of thing. You, surely, would be the best person to fill in those details."

Her ruffled feelings soothed by this, Gussie said, "Well, if you put it that way..." She smiled at Carol. "And will *you* be conducting my interview personally?"

A sudden eruption of sound snatched the attention of everyone in the area. "I demand to see someone in authority!"

Major Hawk, his face flushed an apoplectic brick-red, his mustache seeming to bristle with a life of its own, was pounding on the reception desk with one meaty fist. On the opposite side a young woman tried to quieten him down with a moderate reply. It was to no avail: He repeated his emphatic request, every word accompanied by a heavy blow to the desk in front of the attendant.

"Willoughby!" Before Carol or Bourke could get to their feet, Gussie had rushed over to him and seized his free hand. "Please calm down. You're making a spectacle of yourself."

Wrenching himself away, he bellowed at her, "Murderer!"

Carol and Bourke reached him at the same time. Each taking an arm, they impelled the small man in the direction of the administration offices. "This way, Major," said Bourke. "You need to sit down."

Major Hawk spluttered, "Let me go," but the fire had gone out of him. Tears began to leak from his eyes. "My Fiona," he said. "My Fiona."

When they had him seated in the nearest empty office, and Gussie had been dispatched on the pretext of organizing a bracing cup of tea for the major, Carol said to him, "Why did you call Gussie Whitlew a murderer?"

He knuckled his eyes. A heavy fog of alcohol hung around him, and he seemed not to have changed clothes since the day before. "Gussie's responsible. If she hadn't made Fiona come to play in her bloody Challenge, my daughter would still be with me."

He blew his nose on a crumpled, monogrammed handkerchief. "I've got a case—I've got a case, I know it. I'll sue. She took my daughter away from me, and she'll have to pay for it."

He made an attempt to clutch at Carol's hand, and missed. "You're in charge. You must know all about it. Fiona was fed up with Gussie, fed up with everything. She said she was going to leave, and to hell with the Whitlew Challenge."

"She was going to walk out on the tournament?"

The major shot Bourke an angry glance. "You think she wouldn't do that? You don't know my daughter." At the mention of her name, the tears flowed again. "I really don't know how I'll cope without her."

"Your daughter was serious about leaving before the tournament ended?"

"Serious enough to tell Gussie so, Thursday night. Said she wasn't going to play one more day." He hiccuped forlornly. "We were going to the States together. Las Vegas." His expression turned venomous as he looked through the glass wall at the approaching Gussie. "That is, until *she* killed her."

CHAPTER ELEVEN

After consultation with Carol, Bourke had taken Major Hawk to the tearoom. This was for two reasons: The first was to get him away from Gussie Whitlew, as the major's accusation to her face that she was a murderer had infuriated Gussie to the point of near violence; the second was to sober him up. He'd produced a silver hip flask, declaring, "It's Tanqueray gin—the best."

Bourke had persuaded him to relinquish the flask and was now attempting to cajole Major Hawk into substituting coffee for alcohol, and to eat something to soak up the gin he had already consumed.

Yesterday, after the major's identification of his daughter's body, he'd been too upset for Bourke to get any helpful information, so Carol hoped that a man-to-man conversation over coffee today might be more successful.

Anne Newsome had arrived, full of apologies, and had been dispatched to show the photo of the bracelet around. Carol was now ensconced in Gussie's office, going through the proofs of the Thursday night function with Hilary O'Dell.

"Everybody who is anybody was there," Hilary said. Today her thick, ruddy hair was loose, softening her hooked nose and definite features.

Using a large magnifying glass, Carol examined the photographs closely. Apart from the golfers participating in the Whitlew Challenge, Carol recognized the Lord Mayor of Sydney and several state politicians dancing attendance on the Premier of New South Wales—all smiling toothy, political smiles. There were also stars from sports other than golf, one stellar movie actor, and a gaggle of television personalities. "Quite a turnout," she said.

Gussie Whitlew was everywhere, smiling widely. Fiona Hawk was also featured in many of the photographs, not only with dignitaries, but once in an obviously intense exchange with Eddie Altunga, then in another similar conversation with Gussie, followed by dialogues with Ashleigh Piddock, an Asian woman Hilary identified as Beth Shima, and, in the last set of photographs, Uta Dahlberg.

"I figure," said Hilary, "that I took this last group of photos around eight to eight-thirty, and Fiona's in several of them, so she hadn't left the reception at that point."

Raising her eyebrows at this observation, Carol said, "You didn't happen to notice when she actually did leave, did you?"

"No, but not long before she disappeared, I did see her make a phone call on her mobile, and she had the strangest reaction to the outcome."

"What do you mean?"

"I was calculating how many shots I had left, and had decided not to put in a fresh roll of film, and, as Gussie had instructed me to feature Fiona in as many shots as possible, I was watching out for her. When I caught sight of her, she had an odd expression on her face. She went over to a corner, presumably not to be disturbed, and made a phone call."

"What was odd about her expression?"

"Of course, Inspector, you never had an opportunity to meet Fiona, but if you had, you'd know she was always totally sure of herself. But this time she looked…" Hilary thought for a moment. "She looked disconcerted."

"Did you happen to notice if she dialed the number from memory, or did it seem to be preset on the phone?"

Hilary smiled. "You ask the damnedest questions, Inspector. I was interested enough to watch Fiona closely, and, in fact, she checked a bit of paper before she punched the numbers in."

"What happened then?"

"One of those tiresome would-be actors started badgering me about getting copies of the photos I'd taken at the reception and I lost sight of Fiona, but not before I saw her expression after she made the call. It was hard to describe—sort of angry joy. That's the last—"

Hilary broke off as Davy Vere strode into the office. Hands on hips, he said to Carol, "You wanted to see me?"

Today he was wearing skintight black jeans and plain black T-shirt. Carol thought that if Uta Dahlberg looked dangerous, Davy had an aura of serious, break-your-bones menace. His bleached yellow hair didn't lighten his intimidating expression, and his hard, muscular body promised that whatever he might threaten, he could carry out with ease.

Hilary O'Dell got hastily to her feet. "I'll leave the proofs with you, Inspector Ashton. If there's anything else…"

Davy smirked as she left the office. Carol regarded him with close attention until he demanded, "What?"

"Do you know Hilary O'Dell well?"

"Why?"

"I got the impression she was wary of you."

He showed his teeth in a brief, wolfish smile. "Wary?" he said. "Try scared." He grabbed the back of a chair and swung it around so he could straddle it. "Or maybe she's bloody terrified. You'll have to ask her."

Idly tapping her pen, Carol said, "And the reason for this terror is…?"

"She took a few photos Gussie didn't like. I persuaded O'Dell that selling them to a media outlet would be unwise."

After looking at him for a long moment, Carol asked, "Is it your usual practice to frighten people into agreeing to do whatever you're asking?"

He rested his forearms along the back of the chair in a pose plainly designed to signal his indifference to Carol's questions and her opinion of him. She wondered why he didn't have tattoos—they seemed to go with his persona. Perhaps, she thought with cool amusement, he did, but the tattoos weren't accessible to public view.

"It seems I intimidate people," he said, his smirk reappearing. "I've no idea why."

"Did you find out whether Kasha London's locker had been broken into?"

"What?"

"Yesterday Ms. Whitlew asked you to check Ms. London's locker because she thought someone might have been through her things."

"She'd be lucky," Vere muttered, then added in a louder voice, "I looked into it. There was nothing wrong with her locker. All her imagination."

Carol passed him the photo of the bracelet. "Have you seen this bracelet before?"

He gave it a cursory glance, then flicked the photo onto the desk. "Not that I remember. Why are you asking?"

"Just a routine question." Carol opened her notebook and unscrewed the top of her gold pen. "Who caddied for Fiona Hawk on Thursday?"

"When Ivanovich bailed out on her, I set her up with Mick Slane. He's a topnotch amateur player, and he knows the course well."

After getting details of how to contact the substitute caddie, Carol said, "I've been told you had more than a casual interest in Fiona Hawk."

"So? In case you haven't noticed, she was sexy, famous, and loaded. Why wouldn't I have a go?"

"So you did make advances to her?"

He gave a contemptuous grunt. "Why don't you say what you mean? I wanted to fuck her. So did she want to fuck me?"

"Admirably direct," said Carol. "And did she?"

He lifted his shoulders in a shrug. "She made it clear she wasn't interested. Her loss."

"When was this?"

Davy Vere yawned, making it obvious that he was bored with Carol and her questions. "Not sure."

"Would it have been Thursday? The last day of her life?"

"What's that supposed to mean?"

"It's a question, Mr. Vere. When did you have this conversation with Fiona Hawk?"

He made an angry gesture. "Jesus Christ, you don't give up, do you? I had nothing to do with bashing her head in and arranging her body in the sandpit. And in case you're thinking I know too much about it, so do half the people at the country club. Joe Gallagher's been dining out on the story ever since he found her in the bunker."

Inexorable, Carol said, "I'll ask you again. When did you have this conversation with Ms. Hawk where she made it clear she wasn't interested in you?"

Patches of red showed on his pale cheeks. He sat up erect, his eyes narrow slits. "I don't know," he snapped, "sometime Thursday afternoon. I caught up with her after she'd had the row with Syncomm. She was furious, I can tell you—and she was sexy as hell when she was angry. Got me hard, straightaway."

This last admission apparently pleased Vere, as he relaxed, giving Carol a smug smile.

"I'm looking for a time frame here, Mr. Vere. I believe the day's play ended around four in the afternoon and she was one of the last to finish. How long after that did you speak with her?"

He gave an irritated grunt. "I had to check arrangements for getting the course ready for the next day, and make sure the TV people were happy with everything. Of course the bastards weren't, so it would have been around five or five-thirty when I fronted Fiona. Offered to buy her a drink, but she wasn't keen. No point in wasting time if there was no payoff in the offing, so I put it to Fiona, direct. She said thanks, but no thanks."

"Did she laugh at you?"

He lifted his chin. "No one laughs at me."

Carol gave him a little smile. "What, never?"

She was fascinated to see his nostrils flare and half expected to see him explode in anger, but with an obvious effort, he kept control, saying tightly, "I've told you—Fiona made it clear she wasn't interested. It was no big deal."

"If it was no big deal, then why was it necessary for you to pressure Ruth Gallant to change her story?"

His lip lifting in a sneer, he said, "You've been listening to gossip from a disaffected employee."

"Would you answer my question, please?"

"I've forgotten what it is," he said insolently.

Carol said patiently, "Why did you find it necessary to intimidate Ruth Gallant into changing her story?"

Her persistence got her a noisy sigh. "I was simply trying to save you from running off in the wrong direction," he said. "One of the other attendants told me Ruth had shot off her mouth to you, big-noting herself and making out she knew everything that was going on. All I did was have a word with her to get her to tell the truth."

"Well," said Carol, "she's done that."

"Good."

"Not so good, Mr. Vere, because her account contradicts yours. And I wonder if I ask around if I might not find other people who agree with her."

"Christ! Give it a rest."

"Fiona Hawk was brutally murdered. I'm not giving anything a rest until I find the culprit. That means I'll ask questions until I get answers."

There was real animosity on Davy Vere's face. "I've got work to do," he said. "You're holding me up."

"You'll be out of here much more quickly if you cooperate."

"Look, Fiona was up herself," he said scornfully. "Thought she was a bloody princess. I wasn't good enough for her, and she told me so. I made it clear I didn't like it, but there are plenty more where she came from, so it didn't really worry me."

Carol said, "What were you doing in Melbourne last night?"

Davy Vere had half risen, apparently ready to go. He sank back onto the chair. "What?"

Carol repeated the question. His face stone, he said, "It was confidential work for Gussie. You'll have to ask her about it."

"How would you categorize your duties with Ms. Whitlew?"

"I'm her assistant."

"I believe you've been described as her enforcer."

"You think I strong-arm people for her? No way. I don't want any trouble with the law."

"You have been arrested before, Mr. Vere."

"Yeah. Misunderstandings."

"You have one conviction," said Carol. "That wasn't a misunderstanding, was it?"

Vere got to his feet. "I've got work to do."

"Ruth Gallant is worried about her job. I gather you implied that she would lose it if she didn't say what you wanted her to."

"She's mistaken."

"I trust so," said Carol. "Threatening potential witnesses is a crime. I hope you realize that fact, because if you don't, it's very likely there will be an addition to your arrest record."

She waited until he got to the door before adding, "And, Mr. Vere, I will require a formal, signed statement. Sergeant Bourke will be contacting you on the matter. I'd appreciate it if you kept yourself available."

* * *

After the provoking presence of Davy Vere, Kasha London was a soothing antidote. She shook hands with Carol, made a few remarks about the weather and the luxury of the country club surroundings, then sat with hands folded in her lap, apparently ready to answer all and any questions. She was dressed for play in dark brown shorts and a beige polo shirt, and Carol noticed the placement of the logo and name of a multinational food company on her sleeve and right breast.

Apart from her voice, which was unusually melodious, Kasha London was unremarkable, although a glint of humorous intelligence showed in her eyes.

When they had met briefly yesterday in the reception area, Kasha had impressed Carol with her agreeable, easygoing manner, but at times like this, when Carol felt she might tend to underestimate a witness, she always reminded herself that even the worst of sociopaths was capable of disarming with polite, pleasant behavior.

"How is your head?" Carol asked. "I believe you had a migraine."

"I'm much better, but by late yesterday I could hardly see and couldn't even drive back to my hotel. It was plain stupidity on my part, because when the glare out on the course triggered the migraine, I didn't immediately put on my dark glasses." With a self-deprecating smile she added, "Plus the fact that I didn't shoot a good round, so that compounded the misery."

"Tell me how it was that Liam Ivanovich caddied for you yesterday."

Kasha's expression indicated that the question had surprised her. "I can't imagine why that fact is important."

"Mr. Ivanovich would usually caddie for Fiona Hawk."

"Yes but..." Kasha trailed off, apparently disconcerted. "How can I say this? Fiona was...dead. I mean, to put it bluntly, she wouldn't be needing Liam's services."

"You contacted him?"

"Yes, and asked him to hurry over and caddie for me. My usual caddie didn't want to make the trip to Australia, so I was using a local guy, who was fine, but not in Liam's class."

Looking slightly embarrassed, she added, "I didn't like to ask Liam in front of everybody else, because it looked a bit... opportunistic. Gussie's given us all cell phones—it's cute how you Aussies call them mobiles—so I went outside to make the call."

"I'm puzzled, Ms. London," said Carol. "Liam Ivanovich didn't caddie for Fiona Hawk on Thursday, the first day of the tournament, so why would you expect him to be available to you the next day?"

Kasha bit her lip. "Have you spoken to Liam?"

"Please answer the question."

Looking uncomfortable, she said, "Well, I'm breaking a confidence, but Liam had family trouble, and Fiona agreed to release him. But then he found he didn't need to return to Ireland urgently. Liam told me he'd feel a fool going back to Fiona and begging for his job back, so he didn't let her know he was still here."

"Again I'm puzzled. Ms. Hawk seems to have had an excellent chance of winning the Whitlew Challenge, and I understand it would be customary for her caddie to receive ten percent of such a purse. That's one hundred and fifty thousand dollars. Quite a sum of money to give up to avoid embarrassment."

With a faint smile, Kasha said, "I can't pretend to understand the way Liam's mind works. It may have seemed perfectly logical to him."

"You were keen to use Mr. Ivanovich because you expected him to help your game?"

"I don't know, Inspector, if you realize how vital a good caddie can be. He or she not only totes the bag and all the equipment, but is also a sounding board, an advice giver, a support—a person who knows the course possibly better than you do. I always like to discuss difficult shots with my caddie. It's another pair of eyes, another educated opinion. And Liam is the best. The absolute, total best."

"What time was it when you heard that Ms. Hawk was dead?" Carol asked the question matter-of-factly, but it was a key issue, and she watched Kasha London closely.

"The first thing I heard was that she'd withdrawn from the tournament. Of course the place was buzzing with the news that a body had been found on the course, but I didn't connect that with Fiona—why would I? I took it that Fiona couldn't play because she had suddenly become sick, or perhaps had had an accident. I certainly had no idea that she'd been murdered."

"Did you find her withdrawal good news?"

Kasha grinned. "Trick question, Inspector? If I say yes, I'm heartless and, worse, a bad sport. And if I say no, then I'm a liar."

Smiling in turn, Carol said, "Is that a roundabout way of saying you found her absence from the Challenge good news?"

"Fiona is—was—one of the best female golfers in the world." Amusement curved her ups in a this-is-between-us smile. "Please don't quote me on this, but I am always pleased to have less competition vying for the top prize money."

"So who told you she'd withdrawn? And when?"

"Heavens, I'm not exactly sure of the time. As you can imagine, the news went around like lightning in the locker room, especially as Fiona was leading the tournament."

"And you were placed third."

"And I was very happy to be there. On Thursday I had an eagle on the seventeenth, and that got me into the clubhouse one stroke ahead of Ashleigh. She wasn't a bit pleased."

Carol said, "You didn't do as well in yesterday's play."

A look of chagrin crossed Kasha's face. "No, I totally blew it. I was doing okay, but then I double-bogeyed twice on the back nine."

"So Mr. Ivanovich wasn't as much help as you had hoped."

She shrugged. "It wasn't Liam's fault. Frankly, I wasn't on my game. You have days like that."

"And when did you finally learn that Fiona Hawk was dead? When you came back to the clubhouse?"

"Oh no," said Kasha. "Liam told me, out on the course. I wish he hadn't—it upset me." She put up a hand. "Not that I'm using that as an excuse for my poor score."

"Will Mr. Ivanovich continue to caddie for you?"

With obvious regret, Kasha said, "Probably not. I believe he'll complete this tournament with me, but I have no real hope for the future. Frankly, I'm not successful enough for Liam. As you know, caddies get a percentage of prize money, plus

bonuses. I can't rely on getting the big dollars anymore, so..."
She spread her hands.

"How did you get on with Fiona Hawk?"

"Poor Fiona," said Kasha with every evidence of genuine feeling. "Such a terrible thing to happen to her."

Realizing that this was the first convincing expression of sorrow about the victim's death that she had heard so far, Carol said, "Some found her difficult to deal with."

"I've been on the tour a long time, Inspector, and seen it change. There was a friendly, supportive atmosphere, but now everything's much more competitive. The purses are bigger, although apart from the Whitlew Challenge we don't equal the men's prizes or have the same media exposure. We're getting there, though, so a top woman golfer can make a lot of money if she plays the big tournaments."

"I get the impression that Fiona wasn't well-liked. Do you agree with that?"

"She wasn't the easiest person to get along with, but she had the most wonderful golfing skills, and could routinely hit shots I'd give almost anything to achieve. And Fiona had the right temperament on the course—very calm, very focused. She was so successful—some people resent that. I suppose, too, that she was rather arrogant. Certainly she had some definite ideas and wasn't shy about expressing them."

"You got on well with her?"

Kasha gave Carol a warm, rueful smile. "I get on with everyone, Inspector. I'm a wimp—can't stand confrontations."

"Being a wimp is perhaps not the best characteristic for a professional sportswoman," Carol observed dryly.

This remark amused Kasha. "Well, I confess when I'm out on the course with a club in my hands I'm considerably more assertive. I was referring to personal relationships." With a laugh she added, "Ask my ex-husband. I had the bad judgment to marry another wimp, and we fought over who was the weakest. Doomed from the start."

Carol smiled, then said, "You had a long conversation with Fiona at the reception on Thursday night."

"Oh yes," said Kasha, making a face. "She cornered me in the powder room. Fiona was generally unhappy about everything. It happens sometimes, when nothing seems to go right. Liam wasn't caddying for her, she had problems with her agent, Ralph Syncomm, and her father was causing her a lot of worry."

"Major Hawk was worrying her? How?"

"I don't know how true it is, but Fiona said that her father was drinking too much, and—" Kasha broke off, then said, "Look, Inspector, it bothers me to be talking about Major Hawk this way."

"Anything she said before her death could be important."

With obvious reluctance, Kasha went on, "She thought that Ralph and her father were swindling her. I have no idea if they were or not, but I can tell you that she believed it was true and that she was going to get her lawyers on the case."

"I was under the impression she had already initiated legal action."

"I think Major Hawk talked her out of it, the first time around, but then something set her off again."

"Mr. Syncomm assured me," said Carol, "that the dispute arose over an accountant's error and that there was no legal action being taken against him."

Putting up her hands, Kasha said quickly, "I'm only repeating what I was told. It could be wrong. Fiona was in a really odd mood on Thursday night, and she often exaggerated things."

A series of questions about the scene between Fiona and Brinella Altunga on Thursday morning elicited no new information, except for Kasha's clear distaste for Fiona's attitudes. When Carol mentioned the argument between Ralph Syncomm and Fiona on Thursday afternoon, Kasha smiled sardonically. "Agents," she said scornfully. She shook her head. "I could tell you some stories…"

"Your agent is Uta Dahlberg."

"That's right."

"Are you happy with her representation?"

Kasha pursed her lips. "Well," she said after a long pause, "to be honest, I haven't been all that pleased with Uta lately. Most of her attention seems to be directed toward building up a stable of younger sports stars with future potential."

"Successfully?"

"Not as much as she'd like. Uta's got Ashleigh, although I don't think that'll be for long. And I know Uta approached Fiona when she heard there was trouble with Ralph Syncomm, but Fiona had already told me she was going to switch to one of the really big sports agencies. Didn't give me a name, but if you asked me to guess, I'd say it'd be IMG."

Carol gained nothing further, except that when she asked when Kasha had last seen Fiona Hawk, she was told that Kasha remembered her leaving the reception alone, around eight o'clock.

"Inspector, I have to tee off in a few minutes…"

"We'll be asking you to sign a formal statement later this afternoon." Carol handed her the photo of the bracelet found in the bunker. "Before you go, have you ever seen this before?"

Her astonishment plain, Kasha said, "But it's *mine*. Where on earth did you find it?"

CHAPTER TWELVE

After getting a phone call from Vernon Coop to say that he had had several positive identifications for the two boys who'd been on the golf course on Thursday night, and now that he had full names, he was trying to locate them, Carol went with Kasha London to see for herself the locker that Kasha believed someone had opened and gone through.

Seeing the players' area for the second time, Carol decided the very term *locker room* was hardly adequate to describe the opulence of the surroundings, which were comparable to the facilities of a luxury resort or a top-of-the-line health spa or gym.

Kasha showed Carol her locker, which actually was a burnished metal, custom-made cabinet of generous size. It was opened with a plastic keycard, which was slipped into a slot to activate the electronic mechanism. Carol saw that each locker was labeled with an enamel plate bearing the person's name. The system was alphabetical, so that Toni Karstares's locker was situated to the left of Kasha London's, and Patti Millican's was on the right.

"How's it going?" said Toni Karstares, who was seated nearby changing her shoes.

"The investigation, you mean?" said Carol, noticing again the extraordinary blue of Toni Karstares's eyes.

"Well, yes," she said with a mischievous grin. "I'd hesitate to ask you anything more personal."

"Then I have to assure you that we are pursuing our inquiries." Carol delivered the cliché lightly.

"Are you getting ready to arrest someone?" Toni laughed as she stood and stretched. "You understand my interest—it could be *me*."

"Why would you say that?" Kasha interposed. "Don't even joke about it, Toni. There's every chance that someone we all know *is* the murderer."

Toni shrugged, then walked away with a loose, long-legged stride. Looking after her, Kasha said, "I don't feel safe around here anymore. It could be any of us, unless..." She looked hopefully at Carol. "It's in the news all the time, how some complete stranger kills someone whose name they don't even know."

Carol said, "We're taking all eventualities into account," thinking that she couldn't point out how extremely unlikely it was that a stranger would have access to Brinella's club, or that such a person could arrange for Kasha's bracelet to be found with the body.

Not looking at all reassured, Kasha turned back to her locker. "I hate the idea that someone's been through my things."

"Are you absolutely sure someone has?"

Unsettled, Kasha said, "Maybe I didn't close the door properly. We all know each other, and I suppose we get a bit careless."

Carol flipped the keycard over in her fingers. It was a white plastic rectangle with *Whitlew Country* Club inscribed in red script. "You were only given one card?"

"Yes, but I'm sure there's a master keycard that will open everything. I mean, there has to be."

"Why didn't you report your bracelet missing when you thought someone had been through your locker?"

Kasha made a face. "I'm a bit careless with jewelry, I'm afraid. Always misplacing things and finding them later. And I don't wear bracelets or rings when I'm playing. I think I half remember wondering where the bracelet was, but I was sure it would turn up somewhere, maybe in my hotel room. Actually, until you showed me the photo, I didn't know for sure that it was gone."

"So it could have been taken from your hotel room?"

"Sure." She bit her lip. "Inspector, I have to ask you again where did you find my bracelet? Is it something to do with Fiona? Please—I have to know."

"I'm sorry. I'll tell you as soon as I can.

The area was crowded with players also preparing to go out onto the course, and seeing Brinella Altunga, Carol excused herself and went over to speak with the young Aboriginal woman.

In person she was quite striking, with clear brown skin, dark eyes, and the supple, lithe grace that Carol always associated with professional runners. On the sleeve of her shirt was the red-and-green Dandon logo.

"I'm Detective Inspector Carol Ashton."

Brinella nodded slowly. "I know who you are. Have you spoken with Eddie? He told me to make sure he was with me if you were going to interview me."

Although she intended to extract at least some information now, Carol said, "I'd very much like to talk with you after you finish this afternoon."

"All right, but I don't know anything."

Carol said pleasantly, "That's what your brother said, but there are some routine questions we're asking everyone, and you can't be an exception."

Brinella gave her a faint smile. "I suppose not."

"One thing I would like to ask," said Carol, noticing that the young woman immediately became wary at the possibility of a question, "where are your clubs kept?"

Brinella frowned, puzzled. "My clubs? Eddie usually keeps them with him. But this clubhouse has a terrific equipment room, where you can clean everything, make repairs, and then lock everything away safely, so we've been leaving my stuff here."

"You use Dandon clubs?"

Now Brinella really was on guard. "Yes," she said, watching Carol closely. "The company just became my main sponsor."

Thinking that Brinella was rather like a filly ready to bolt, Carol said in a tone of mild inquiry, "I believe that pro golf players have their clubs specifically tailored. Is that right?"

Brinella, although still vigilant, relaxed a little at Carol's conversational tone. "For professionals, clubs are customized for height, arm length, and swing speed."

Bourke had said that the sand wedge was a professional, customized club. "How interesting. Would you mind explaining?"

Keen enthusiasm lit Brinella's eyes, and Carol realized that this was the best possible way to get this young woman talking—start off with golf.

"I'm tall," said Brinella, "so I have a more upright swing, and that affects the lie of the club." She smiled. "I'm getting a bit technical here, but that's to do with the angle between the head of the club and the shaft. As for arm length, it's pretty obvious how that makes a difference to how long the shaft of the club is."

To show her interest, and to keep Brinella talking, Carol said, "And swing? Is that to do with how high you lift the club before you hit the ball?"

Brinella shook her head. "Not, it's not that. It's how *hard* you swing at the ball. Average players use clubs with flexible shafts to help them hit a long way, but clubs like that aren't very accurate. Most pros use stiff or extra-stiff steel shafts, because they swing at the ball hard enough to get the distance, and stiff shafts give more accuracy."

"So all your clubs are Dandon brand?"

Brinella frowned at this more specific question, obviously wondering where this was going. "Not exactly. All my irons are Dandon, but I've got a favorite putter that's made by another company."

"What about your sand wedge?"

"Yes, it's a Dandon." She was openly suspicious now. "Why are you asking me about my clubs?"

"I was wondering if it's possible that one could be missing."

Mystification was rapidly giving way to alarm. "This is about Fiona, isn't it? Something to do with what happened to her?"

"I'd rather not say. Could we check your bag now?"

Brinella stared at her, eyes wide. "Eddie's in the equipment room getting everything ready."

Carol gestured for Brinella to lead the way. "Please. This will only take a moment."

* * *

Hugh Haver had delivered another copy of his report, and Carol asked one of the office staff to make her an extra copy. Before she read it she put a call through to Leota's hotel. She half expected that she would be switched to voice mail, but Leota's warm voice answered the phone.

"I didn't think I'd catch you," Carol said, smiling.

"Well you have caught me, Carol, so what are you going to do with me now?"

"Not much, I'm afraid," said Carol, wishing she could continue a playful conversation but conscious that she had very little time. "I'm calling to tell you I can't guarantee when I'll get away from here."

She had hoped to pick up Leota from her hotel so that they could have a quiet dinner together at Carol's place, but the way the investigation was developing made that delightful idea unlikely.

"Tell you what," said Leota, "come here to the hotel when you can. It doesn't matter what time, or if you wake me up." She chuckled. "In fact, I'd love to have you break into my slumbers."

Carol jotted down the room number, anticipation warming her. After she broke the connection she called her neighbor to ask for Sinker to be fed, then sat down to read through the copy of Hugh Haver's report. She had only just started when Mark Bourke came in.

"Did you hear the sirens?" he asked, grinning.

"Aunt Sarah and her Eco-Crones?" she asked, resigned to the answer.

Bourke chuckled. "Aunt Sarah and her ecology gang," he confirmed. "I popped outside the clubhouse to have a look. She and her Eco-Crones are stirring up a lot of interest. There're two patrol cars, TV trucks, and quite a sizable crowd providing an appreciative audience. When I left, your aunt was fluttering around in a very colorful outfit."

"Street theater," said Carol. "She's playing a poisoned butterfly."

Bourke looked at her, and they both laughed. "Oh, for a relative like that," said Bourke. "Mine are all so bland."

"Bland is good." She sighed. "I have a premonition I'll be bailing her out later today."

"If that's necessary, I'll get Pat to talk with Sybil. One of them can arrange bail—I don't think either of us needs the distraction."

"Is Pat here yet?" said Carol, remembering belatedly that Bourke's wife was going to be a tournament spectator today.

"She's already on the course checking out the best vantage points. I told her to look out for you, just in case you had time to grab a coffee with her."

"I doubt I will." She smiled at Bourke. "Mark, you look all majored-out," she said. "Was Willoughby Hawk worth the effort? Did he give any more reasons why he found it necessary to make a public announcement that Gussie Whitlew was a murderer?"

"Gussie is Major Hawk's principal suspect in his daughter's death because, if I may quote him, 'Gussie has unnatural urges.'"

"That's it?"

"Pretty well, but he was more helpful about Ralph Syncomm," said Bourke. "I'm starting to believe the suspicion Fiona had about her father and Syncomm being in cahoots is basically true. Sloshed or not, Hawk was coherent enough to cheerfully implicate Ralph Syncomm in financial chicanery, whilst making a fair attempt to exonerate himself from any wrongdoing."

"Suspicions are all very well, but did you get anything concrete?" Carol asked.

"Enough to know what questions to ask about her financial affairs. I'd say Syncomm will be in deep trouble if any detailed investigation of his representation is carried out."

"And her father's part in all this?"

"Put brutally, he's a grade-A sponger. And yes, Fiona had given him his marching orders, although he seems sure he could have persuaded her to relent, like he has a dozen times before. You know, I find myself feeling a bit sorry for him. He's lost his meal ticket and his daughter in one blow."

"Speaking of blows," said Carol, "it looks as if Brinella Altunga's Dandon sand wedge *is* the murder weapon. It's missing from her golf bag, and the two other players both still have theirs."

Remembering the scene in the equipment room, Carol grimaced. "I don't think Brinella really understood the ramifications of the missing club, but Eddie certainly did— he put two and two together and became predictably rabid, alternating between accusing me, various other competitors, and Gussie Whitlew of deliberately trying to implicate his sister in Fiona's murder. Then Brinella cried—sobbed, actually. There was quite a crowd in the equipment room, and although I tried to keep Eddie Altunga quiet, he made so much noise about

Brinella's missing club that everybody there leapt to the correct conclusion that it had been used to kill Fiona Hawk."

"Someone is trying to implicate her," said Bourke, "that is, unless she's dumb enough to leave one of her clubs at the scene."

"I can imagine her panicking, and leaving something incriminating behind, but the club was used precisely, and then carefully arranged. I don't think she's a convincing suspect."

"What about her brother?"

"He's very protective. He might well be capable of violence, but I don't think he'd do anything to throw suspicion on his sister."

After Eddie had calmed down, he'd told Carol that he had cleaned and checked the equipment—and all the clubs were there—before putting everything away in a steel cabinet, far less lavish than those in the players' area. "Another electronic lock," said Carol, "and opened by the same keycard as Brinella uses for her personal locker."

"There's a master?"

"More than one. Security isn't one of the Whitlew Country Club's areas of excellence. Several people have master keys, including Davy Vere, the person heading the administrative staff, and Gussie herself. There's even a master key available to the cleaners, as long as they sign for it."

Carol mentioned that Vernon Coop had called, saying he believed the boys had been identified, and would call as soon as he picked them up. She then briefly covered her interviews with Davy Vere and Kasha London. "She says the bracelet is definitely hers, but she can't remember when she last saw it, which isn't much help."

Bourke put his hands behind his head and leaned back in his chair. "What a case. We have a victim who has more enemies than friends, a suspect list that's growing, and a wide-open time of death, so that practically everyone seems to have had the opportunity to do murder. Plus we have two items possibly planted at the crime scene to incriminate innocent parties. And, of course, no fingerprints or witnesses."

Imitating Bourke's jocular tone, Carol said, "Fiona Hawk, who is attractive, talented, and rich, spends Thursday rubbing various people up the wrong way, as well as shooting sixty-four to come in eight under par, thus making herself the leader for the first day of the Whitlew Challenge."

"Quite an achievement," said Bourke, "and as the purse for this tournament is an astonishing one-and-a-half million, Fiona's excellent round is likely to be the subject of hidden angst, rather than admiration, as far as many of the other competitors are concerned."

"I think you're being unfair, Mark. She might not have been liked, but she was widely admired as a golfer."

"The person who killed her didn't admire her," remarked Bourke. "To continue Fiona goes to the reception Gussie's throwing at the conclusion of the first day's play. Both her father and her agent avoid her, Eddie Altunga delivers some harsh words, Fiona complains mightily to Kasha London about her life in general, then she makes a mysterious phone call and leaves the reception somewhere between eight and nine."

"What puzzles me," said Carol, "is why she's out on the golf course at night. What would persuade her to do that?"

"Love?" said Bourke. "Or hate?" He stared at the ceiling for inspiration. "Now, where were we? Fiona leaves the function, possibly alone, between eight and nine, and meets up with someone with whom she has a heated argument on the way to the headland near the fourth hole."

He got up and made a few preparatory swings with an imaginary golf club. "In the light of the moon she's knocked unconscious, her assailant arranges her neatly in the middle of the bunker, and with Brinella Altunga's sand wedge"—he mimicked someone preparing for a shot—"takes a mighty swing at Fiona's skull, killing her with a single blow."

Carol thought of the full moon shining down, turning the red blood black on the white sand. "What time did the moon come up on Thursday?"

"By eight it was high in the sky. No clouds. No wind. A perfect night."

They sat silently for a moment. Bourke, suddenly somber, said, "Brutal, and premeditated. Not a heat-of-the-moment thing. That makes this one very dangerous, Carol."

She nodded, then handed him Haver's report. "I made a copy, so we can check it through together."

After a moment Bourke laughed. "He gets coffee, he takes a leak, and he tells you all about it!"

Carol didn't respond. Looking up, Bourke said, "What is it?"

"The bottom of page two. Haver sees a yellow Porsche parked with the lights off. He drives past, and when he comes back, it's gone."

"So?"

Carol said, "Gussie Whitlew has a yellow Porsche."

CHAPTER THIRTEEN

"I don't suppose, Inspector, that I can tempt you to join me out on the course to watch some of the play."

"That'd be a great idea. Thank you."

Clearly astonished at Carol's immediate acceptance of her invitation, Gussie said, "Why that's ...wonderful."

Over her head, Bourke winked at Carol. "I'll hold the fort here," he said.

If Gussie Whitlew had not conveniently asked, Carol had been prepared to initiate an informal meeting. There were many questions for her to answer, and Carol had decided that an apparently casual conversation would be the most effective way to catch Gussie off guard.

"Thanks, Mark," Carol said, leaving him to chase down phone records, to contact the Irish police to check on Liam Ivanovich's family situation, and also to interview Mick Slane, the substitute caddie Fiona had used on Thursday. Anne Newsome had obtained an up-to-date staff list for the country club and was running a criminal activity check on all the names.

Terry Roham had been dispatched to follow up on the search for Justin Mott and Ken Lawson, both boys having been absent from their homes this morning when Coop's officers arrived to interview them.

Gussie set off toward the rear of the clubhouse at a brisk pace. She had exchanged her high heels for her white-and-tan golf shoes and was a diminutive figure next to Carol. "Have you been out to the front of the club in the last few hours?" she asked. "Your aunt and her cronies have stirred up quite a lot of trouble."

"I haven't seen the demonstration."

Gussie grinned up at her. "Ashamed of your relative, are you? I know what you mean—I have nothing whatsoever to do with Burt's side of the family since his death. They hate me anyhow, since they got peanuts in Burt's will."

The story of the Whitlew fashion house was well known. Established by the young husband-and-wife team of Burt and Gussie Whitlew, it had grown over the years from a small clothing factory to a hugely successful international company, largely due to the brilliance of Gussie's creative abilities, backed by her husband's equally impressive financial skills. There had been rumors that the marriage was in trouble, fueled by Gussie's forays into the gay world, but their union had endured the gossip. Then, five years ago, Burt had suffered the last of a series of heart attacks. His will had been bitterly contested by his family, but Gussie had emerged victorious and had proceeded to take Whitlew Fashions on to even greater prosperity.

"I'm not ashamed of Aunt Sarah," said Carol. "I'm proud of her. She stands up for what she believes in."

Gussie seemed to be about to make some scathing remark, but a look at Carol's face apparently convinced her to change the subject. "That's a *much* better color on you, Inspector," she said, eyeing Carol's cobalt blue tunic top. "One of mine, I believe?"

Carol smiled. "I think it is."

This morning she'd done an unaccustomed check of clothing labels in her wardrobe and had been amused to find that this particular top had a red GUSSIE on its label, designating it a garment from the Whitlew collection. She'd decided to team it with cream slacks and had remarked to Sinker, who was curled up snoozing on the bed, that she was dressing for success—at least with regard to interviewing Gussie Whitlew.

"I'd love to have the chance to choose some clothes for you," Gussie said, sizing Carol up with a professional frown. "You've got the carriage, the figure, to wear something dramatic, striking."

"I don't need to be dramatic and striking in my line of work."

"Oh, I'm not talking about *work*. I'm talking about your *life*. Your personal style. Your impact on the world. And don't look amused, Inspector—fashion is serious business."

"I can see that."

Carol's dry tone caused a flicker of irritation to cross Gussie's perfectly made-up face. She calmed herself by patting her streaked-blond hair. "Many women would give their right arms to have Gussie Whitlew offer to dress them," she declared.

"Missing right arms would make choosing clothes for them rather a challenge, wouldn't it?" asked Carol ingenuously.

Gussie gave a shout of laughter. "Oh, good one!"

Her humor restored, Gussie led Carol to a large electric golf cart that had obviously been custom built for her. Designed to carry four, it was painted gold, with a red *Gussie Whitlew* in script on the side panel. The roof was black, with gold tassels at each corner.

"The compartment on the left is refrigerated and carries champagne and other cold drinks, should you want them," said Gussie, obviously proud of her vehicle. "The other side holds coffee, salads, and things to nibble. Would you like anything before we start?"

Carol declined, wondering what sort of driver Gussie would be without the raw power of a Porsche or a Ferrari. She didn't have long to wait for an answer, as almost before she had sunk into the softness of the black leather seat, Gussie had the golf cart darting out of the covered area and onto the course. "I can break all my own rules," she said. "No one else is permitted to speed the way I do, or to go off the marked paths."

"One of the perks of being at the top," said Carol, hanging on as Gussie, hardly slowing, bumped off the path to make a detour around a group of spectators who were making their way between holes.

Snatching up a walkie-talkie from between the front seats, Gussie mumbled into it for a few moments. She slapped it back into its holder, announcing, "Toni's still leading, but only by one shot. She's playing with Ashleigh, and they're on the ninth. It's a par four, tricky, with a dogleg right, narrow fairway squeezed by trees, water directly in front of the green, and three bunkers protecting the hole."

"Sounds formidable."

Gussie shot her a wicked smile. "Binnie Bayline can be positively fiendish when designing a golf course, and my instructions were, Break those little golfing hearts. That makes the Whitlew Country Club a real challenge, even for the top players."

The golf cart slowed as the path climbed to a high point of the course. Gussie pulled over and leaned out to scan the sky. "There's a possibility of a severe storm—thunder and lightning. At least, that's the latest forecast for the afternoon. It's a worry, because being out in the open, especially with metal clubs, makes everyone a lightning-strike candidate."

The view from their aspect was spectacular. The course was a series of verdant billows, ornamented by a tracery of trees and greenery. Water hazards scintillated in the brilliant sunlight. High up, wheeling seagulls decorated the arch of the pale sky. Carol could see, off to their left, the blue of the ocean, dotted with white sails.

Gussie concentrated on the southern sky. "Do you think it's getting dark over there? I can't afford a suspension in play, especially with a live telecast involved." She narrowed her eyes, as though this would make it possible for her to see farther. "You know a southerly can whip up the coast in a matter of minutes."

She started the cart and zoomed down a long incline at what seemed to Carol breakneck speed. "I've taken precautions, of course. Got air horns set up to warn everybody if a storm is approaching."

They rocketed around a curve, scattering a few stray spectators. Carol said, "On Thursday night your yellow Porsche was seen parked on the perimeter road, down toward the cliffs, around eleven o'clock."

"*My* yellow Porsche? Surely you mean *a* yellow Porsche."

"Why were you there?"

"I wasn't."

Gussie wasn't asking the obvious questions, and she wasn't protesting enough. Carol smiled grimly. "You're not surprised by this topic, are you?"

Her expression guileless, Gussie said, "I don't know what you mean."

"If Davy Vere had broken into my briefcase, I imagine it would have been a neat job. What did you use? A screwdriver? A knife?"

Gussie looked at Carol, then her face broke into a smile. She threw up one hand and laughed. "A screwdriver I found in Davy's desk drawer. I never was good with tools, and I nearly broke a nail." She added with a chuckle, "Are you going to arrest me?"

"How did you know to even look for Haver's report?"

"Steve told me—you've met Steve, he's security on the front gate. Hughie, I believe the young cop calls himself, complained bitterly to Steve about how you'd demanded that he write a detailed report of everything that happened while he was on patrol. I hoped he hadn't bothered to mention my car, but of course he's a petrol-head, and noticed it because it's the latest model Porsche."

Her lips curved in a mischievous smile, she went on. "You would have hooted if you'd seen me in action. I checked the desk—you'd left nothing there—then found your briefcase. I rushed off, found a screwdriver, and hurried back, terrified that someone would walk in on me in the middle of a burglary.

It was quite fun, really. Once I'd got the lock open, I went through everything, grabbed the report, and was about to make a photocopy of it, when I heard the cleaners coming into the admin offices. Of course I could have bluffed my way out of it, but Carol—I'm sorry, *Inspector*—I was so into the role of burglar that I pushed the briefcase lock hard until it clicked, and then, heart pounding, I got out of there."

She slowed the golf cart and pulled over to park it not far from a large assembly of spectators. Turning to Carol, her face alive with laughter, Gussie said, "You know, for a moment or two, it was almost as exciting as sex."

Repressing a reluctant smile, Carol said coolly, "Why were you there at eleven o'clock at night?"

"Being a fool, basically. Fiona said she'd meet me at my beach house after the reception. My place is about twenty minutes from here—I'd love you to see it."

"Please keep to the point."

No longer amused, Gussie's face was showing a mixture of annoyance and embarrassment. She said, "During the evening, I talked with Fiona. She was asking about her bonus—she'd come in first for the day and she was keen to know when she'd get paid. I sweet-talked her—at least I thought I did—into coming back to my place."

"With the aim of?"

"Seducing her, of course." Gussie shot a defiant look in Carol's direction. "Fiona was an adult. She made her own decisions."

"What happened?"

"When I was ready to leave the reception, Fiona had already gone. She'd been to my place before, so I expected she'd be waiting there. I drove straight home, but no Fiona. Gave her about twenty minutes and, when she didn't turn up, I came back to the club."

"Why did you think she'd be down near the cliffs?"

"We'd walked there before, on Wednesday afternoon after Fiona played a practice round. She said she'd love to come back and see the cliffs and ocean by moonlight. I guessed that there was a chance she'd be there."

"By herself?"

Gussie's face clouded. "No, I thought she'd probably had a better offer, so she'd certainly be with someone."

"Anyone in particular?"

Gussie's mouth turned down. "Probably male, certainly attractive. Maybe one of the waiters."

"Did you see her?"

"No. And I realized I was behaving like a total idiot, chasing after her like that. Too late I remembered that the perimeter road was being patrolled. I got out of there fast, but obviously not fast enough."

The way Gussie told it, her story was, at least on the surface, convincing, but Carol had heard a thousand convincing stories before, and many had turned out to be false, if not in total, certainly in the details.

They got out of the cart and walked over to join the crowd. The players were close to the ninth hole flag. Toni Karstares's ball rested at the edge of the rough on the other side of the large water hazard that guarded the green from the fairway. Ashleigh Piddock, who'd hit to the right of the water, had a shorter distance to cover, as her ball was near the lip of the largest of the three sand traps ringing the green.

The spectators, held in check by marshals and a rope barrier, watched with close attention as Toni Karstares studied her next shot and conferred with her caddie. Gussie said in a piercing whisper, "Toni's caddie is the professional here at the country club, and he will be the one giving you lessons—that is, if you care to take me up on my offer."

Carol's patient, not-this-subject-again smile put a frown on Gussie face, but she soon recovered to say, "Toni's got the harder task. She's got to do a flop shot, whereas Ashleigh just has a bump and run."

"Quiet, please," said a marshal, holding up a sign with the same words.

"She's using a wedge," Gussie whispered. "Feet close together, stance open…Oh, good shot!"

The ball flew very high, cleared the water, and dropped nearly straight down, rolling only a short distance until it stopped within a meter of the hole.

Murmurs of appreciation were accompanied by polite clapping. Then all attention turned to Ashleigh Piddock. The marshal repeated his command to be quiet, although Carol thought this hardly seemed necessary with such a polite, interested crowd.

Chewing gum all the while, Ashleigh studied the lie of her ball, squinted at the hole, then took the club her caddie was holding out to her and made a few preparatory swings.

"Her short game is wonderful," confided Gussie, gaining a *shh* from a man nearby.

Ashleigh hit the ball crisply. It took a low hop and then ran onto the green. Now that the golfer's concentration could not be broken, noise swelled from the spectators as the ball continued to roll toward the flag, culminating in a muted cheer when it dropped into the hole.

"If Toni sinks her putt, they'll be coleaders," said Gussie, thrilled. "A close competition! It's ideal for television."

Toni dutifully tapped her ball into the hole, and the spectators started moving—some to watch the players tee off, others hurrying to strategic positions along the fairway or at the next green.

"There are these ridiculous, archaic rules for golf clothing," said Gussie. "I could bring a little fashion into the sport, make it fun—but no, there's no room for innovation. I've approached the LPGA, but I was fobbed off."

She gestured at Toni and Ashleigh. "Look at them—might as well be twins, dressed from a bargain basement. Would you believe, the top must have a collar, no exceptions? So everyone wears a polo shirt in a solid color or unexciting pattern. As for the shorts, they have to be loose and not too far above the knee. The whole outfit is like an uninspired uniform."

"Isn't that Ralph Syncomm?" said Carol.

Gussie looked at him with disfavor. "You'd think he'd at least pretend to feel some sorrow over Fiona's death."

"Perhaps he's good at hiding his feelings," said Carol wryly.

"What Ralph's feeling is relief. With Fiona gone, he's off the hook. Willoughby Hawk certainly won't pursue any legal action against him—it'd be too self-incriminating."

She narrowed her eyes. "I can't stand the man. He's following Ashleigh around, trying to show her how dedicated he'll be to her career if she switches to his agency." She wrinkled her nose, as though smelling something unpleasant. "And I'd say the little twerp is planning to chat up Beth Shima as well, because her contract is up for renewal too."

"Excuse me for a moment," said Carol, "while I have a word with him."

Today Ralph's puny body was clad in designer sports clothes, but the most expensive of attire could not disguise his rounded shoulders and poor posture. His thinning hair was covered by a brown leather cap, and designer dark glasses rode his angular nose.

"Mr. Syncomm?"

"Inspector Ashton—what are you doing here?"

Carol smiled. "Just getting some air. I'd very much like to see you later this afternoon, before you leave the country club."

"I've already told you everything I know."

Carol didn't mind unsettling him a little. She said, "We do have new information. And also I would appreciate you making a formal, signed statement."

His lower lip twitched in a nervous tic. "What about?"

"It's merely to formalize the information you gave me yesterday."

Syncomm wasn't reassured, and Carol was aware that he was staring after her as she returned to Gussie's cart.

Plainly intrigued, Gussie said, "What was all that about?"

Carol raised her eyebrows and was fascinated to see Gussie actually blush. "Sorry," she said with an apologetic smile. "I'm a tyrant, you know, and so used to barking orders that I forget, sometimes, that not everyone is here to obey me."

"Davy Vere obeys you."

Sliding into her seat, she said, "Of course. Otherwise he wouldn't keep his job."

"What was he doing for you in Melbourne?"

Gussie turned her head sharply. "It was a business matter."

"Mr. Vere has been described by several people as your enforcer, and that was, I'm told, the role he was taking when you sent him to Melbourne on Friday."

"I know you've spoken to Davy. What did he say?"

"What do *you* say?"

Gussie looked thoughtful. "Your source of information—it wouldn't be a certain sports writer, would it?"

When Carol didn't answer, she gave an angry snort. "Journalists will do anything for a story, you must know that better than I do. They twist the truth, hint at things in such a way as to skirt the libel laws, and sometimes they tell outright lies."

She looked sideways at Carol. "Was it Mandi Fiedler? Was she complaining about Davy?"

Carol sighed. "Let's be direct. Davy Vere went to Melbourne on your instructions. His task was to neutralize a potentially damaging story about you and Fiona Hawk."

Not bothering to deny that Carol had accurately described her assistant's assignment, Gussie said, "The story was a complete exaggeration. All I did was take steps to protect myself."

"Did Fiona Hawk threaten to leave the tournament?"

"She'd never do that."

"Did she say she would?"

Gussie's face hardened. "I've never made any secret of my interest in women, even when I was married. Fiona knew exactly what the situation was. She was willful, and inclined to make threats she had no intention of carrying out. And when she'd been drinking, the stories got wilder."

She made an irritable, fluttering gesture with one hand. "Fiona was stupid enough to have a drunken conversation with a journalist, and everything gets blown out of proportion. All that I asked Davy to do was to put a stop to the rumors."

"Mandi Fiedler maintains that she didn't repeat what Fiona had told her to anyone."

"Don't tell me you believe her!"

"If you thought she was the source of rumors, why didn't you talk directly with her? She's been at the clubhouse on several occasions."

"I wasn't going to give Fiedler any more material to distort," snapped Gussie. "And I have nothing more to say on the subject."

She started the cart with a jerk. "Let's see some more golf."

Gussie, tight lipped, cut across to the twelfth, where Beth Shima and Brinella Altunga were playing. They joined the crowd close to the commentator, who was whispering into a microphone. *"Brinella Altunga is going with a seven iron for this shot. The hole location is at the back, so she has plenty of green to work with…Good solid shot…Clears the bunker, and onto the green. This player is so good with middle and short irons…It's rolling…rolling…"*

A sigh of disappointment came from the spectators. *"Well,"* said the commentator, *"she has a very long one for birdie, but her putter's magic today…"*

Gussie's mobile phone beeped urgently. She listened for a moment and said, "Are you sure? Yes, then go ahead." She shoved it into her pocket, exclaiming, "Fuck!"

"What is it?"

"Look over there," she said, pointing.

Although they were in calm, bright sunshine, the sky to the south had suddenly become a boiling mass of purplish cloud, extinguishing the blue sky as it raced toward them. Carol felt the initial whisper of cooler air against her face just as she saw the first lightning flicker in the clouds, still too far away to hear the accompanying thunder. The air horns blared a warning, and people scattered for shelter.

"Get into the cart," said Gussie.

"Carol!" It was Pat, Bourke's wife. She was taller than Carol, and moved with a bouncy resilience, as if she had springs in her heels. She embraced Carol, saying in her cheerful, no-nonsense manner, "Let's get out of this bloody storm. I, for one, don't fancy being fried by lightning."

Carol opened her mouth to introduce Pat to Gussie Whitlew, but Gussie forestalled her by saying, "Pat James! You didn't tell me you were coming to the tournament. If you had, I'd have given you the honored-guest treatment."

"You know each other?"

"Of course," said Gussie. She grinned at Pat. "I'm a patron of the arts, aren't I?"

It was no surprise, now that she thought about it, that Gussie should know Pat, who had begun her administrative career at the Art Gallery of New South Wales and had then moved into the private art world, where she was a partner in a successful art gallery.

The three of them fled to Gussie's golf cart as a blast of chilling wind lashed the trees around them, and heavy drops of rain began to fall.

"How do you two know each other?" said Gussie, once they had gained the uncertain shelter of the vehicle.

"I'm married to Mark Bourke."

Gussie was in turn surprised, then thoughtful. "Are you? I had no idea your husband was a policeman."

"Don't make any plans of pumping Pat for information," said Carol lightly.

"I wouldn't dream of it," Gussie declared. She started the cart. "Let's get out of this."

The rain intensified, and overhead lightning crackled and danced, the cracks of thunder crashing almost simultaneously with the each flash. Carol had the thought that this would put a damper on the Eco-Crones for the Environment's protest, and she hoped it was in time to thwart Aunt Sarah's aim of being arrested for the evening news.

As if she had picked up Carol's thought, Pat said, "I saw your aunt in action when I was coming in. Mark says I have to be on hand to bail her out, if necessary."

"Eco-Crones!" Gussie snorted derisively, peering ahead through the gray sheets of rain. "More like *Eco-Clowns*."

Pat started to say something, but a dazzling flash, coinciding with a tremendous clap of thunder, drowned out her words.

Energized, Gussie, eyes wide with excitement, raced the cart toward the clubhouse. "Yippee!" she shouted.

CHAPTER FOURTEEN

The clubhouse was filled with damp people clamoring for drinks, coffee, food. Outside the rain was slackening, and the thunder, though deafening still, came less frequently.

"Let's go into the players' private lounge," said Gussie. Grabbing Pat's right arm and Carol's left, she bustled them through the throng.

It was relatively peaceful in the lounge, although it was rapidly filling with players, caddies, and a few sports writers, Mandi Fiedler among them. Carol saw Kasha come in with Liam Ivanovich, followed by Toni Karstares, who caught Carol's eye and smiled at her.

The players' lounge was another room that demonstrated, Carol thought, Gussie Whitlew's rather unique interior decorating touch. The ceiling and carpet were the same dark blue, the walls pale olive, the lounge chairs and coffee tables a particularly startling shade of lime green. There were four sculptures: At each corner of the room stood an elongated female figure in white marble, each contorted into what seemed to Carol to be a painful pose.

Seeing Carol looking at them, Gussie said with pride, "Each represents one of the four seasons. Do you like them?"

Carol was considering a politic reply when Davy Vere came up to them. Ignoring Pat and Carol, he said to Gussie, "Rain's easing, so we'll have the players back on the course in no time." He jerked his head in the direction of a large television monitor set up high in one corner of the room. "They're doing a tribute to Fiona Hawk to fill in the time."

Gussie didn't looked pleased. "I distinctly told those television people I wanted highlights from the last day's play if we had a rain suspension."

"Don't look at me. I had nothing to do with it." Davy's glance slid to Carol. "You've been on the program already," he said, not hiding his dislike, "a rerun of your media conference. You didn't say much, did you?"

"I didn't intend to."

"Definitely a charmer," said Pat after Vere had walked off. "He works for you, Gussie?"

"My assistant. He's very efficient, but I concede a little lacking in polish."

"A little lacking? He was positively disrespectful to Carol." Pat gave Carol an affectionate half-hug. "And we can't have that, can we?"

"You nasty little man!" came from the other side of the lounge. Conversations died as heads turned.

"Bitch!"

"Oh, God," said Gussie, "not with the media here, especially the Fiedler woman."

Ralph Syncomm, red faced, was standing toe-to-toe with an equally enraged Uta Dahlberg. As she was taller than he, and, with her black hair, pale skin and piercing eyes, far more physically imposing, Syncomm looked rather like a bantam rooster who'd picked an unfortunate fight and couldn't, or wouldn't back down.

Uta Dahlberg's clear voice rang through the room. "You think you can poach Ashleigh from me, do you? Well, think again, you conniving bastard."

"I'd better break this up," said Gussie. "It's not making a good impression."

Pat grinned at Carol. "I wouldn't say that. It seems to be fine entertainment for the assembled multitude."

She was right: The argument had drawn everyone's attention and, although there were some expressions of consternation or disapproval, most people seemed amused, including Ashleigh Piddock. She was sprawled in a lounge chair, one leg negligently dangling over the padded arm, a half-smile on her face.

"Please," said Gussie, stepping between the combatants, "this is hardly the place for a heated business discussion."

"Business discussion?" Uta Dahlberg's tone was scathing. "It's not possible to have a business discussion with a criminal."

Syncomm swelled with rage. "I'll have you in court for that slanderous comment."

Uta Dahlberg swung around to Ashleigh. "You can't be seriously thinking of signing with this creature."

"Nah, I'm not," declared Ashleigh, making circles with her hanging foot. Uta's look of triumph was short-lived, as the young woman went on, "Like, I'm thinking of signing with IMG, or some other big outfit."

This announcement united Ralph Syncomm and Uta Dahlberg in shocked disbelief. "You can't do that," said Uta.

"Yeah, I can."

Gussie took the opportunity to beckon Davy Vere, who unceremoniously propelled the two agents out of the room.

Carol noticed Mandi Fiedler, moving like a shark through water, heading for Ashleigh, who, quite unconcerned, was attempting to blow a pink bubble with her gum.

"Excuse me," said Gussie, trying to deflect Mandi Fielder from her target. "Play is resuming any moment. You can't do an interview now."

"'S all right," said Ashleigh, "Like, I don't mind."

"Inspector Ashton?"

Carol turned to find Eddie Altunga beside her. He looked, for the first time in her experience with him, uncertain. He said, "Do you have a minute?"

"Of course."

He glanced at Pat, and then back to Carol. "Could we speak in private?"

Pat, taking the hint, said, "I'll get something to drink," and left them alone.

Eddie cleared his throat. "First, I want to apologize. I know I was rude to you, and you were only doing your job." He took a deep breath. "I'm not trying to make excuses, but growing up in a little town, people like us didn't get on with the cops. Know what I mean?"

"Yes, I do know what you mean." In some country towns there had been a culture that had fostered ongoing conflict between law enforcement and the black population. Aborigines were generally pushed to the bottom of the social heap and treated as second-class citizens.

Eddie said awkwardly, "Look, Inspector, Brinella trusts everyone—it's one of the nicest things about her—but it means that people try to take advantage, especially as she's a poster girl for Aboriginal success. People are always pestering her—journalists, agents, fans. It never stops. And then there's the hate mail and phone calls, telling us to get back where we came from…I'm there to make sure it doesn't get too much for her."

"Thank you for apologizing, but I assure you I didn't take it personally."

He shuffled his feet. "There's something else. Brinella made me promise to tell you that she thinks Gussie Whitlew might have something to do with the club that's missing from her bag."

"Why would she think that?"

"Gussie was interested in her Dandon equipment. Said that they were a likely sponsor for next year's tournament, and she wanted to know what Brinella thought of the clubs."

"Is that it?"

"No, of course not. Brinella went back to the equipment room after she'd changed on Thursday night, because she'd left her asthma spray in the pocket of her golf bag." Carol watched Eddie's expression change to his familiar truculence. "You won't say anything about the asthma, will you?" he demanded. "Brinella doesn't want anyone to know."

"It's a private medical matter as far as I'm concerned."

He gave her a long stare. "All right, then."

"So your sister went back to the equipment room," Carol prompted.

"There was no one else in there but Gussie, and when she saw Brinella, she acted all guilty, mumbled something, and left in a hurry."

"Brinella didn't actually see anything?"

"She's not making this up."

Carol said, "I'm sure Brinella's telling the truth, but merely seeing Ms. Whitlew in the equipment room of her own country club doesn't mean very much."

"Gussie'd have a master key that'd open every locker, wouldn't she?"

"Did your sister find the locker open?"

"No, and in case you're going to ask, she didn't notice anything wrong. She just got her spray and left."

"Why didn't Brinella come and tell me this herself?"

Eddie gave her a small, tight smile. "She's scared of you." Seeing Carol looking around the room, he said, "Brinella's not here—she doesn't like crowds."

"I would like to talk with her."

Clearly reluctant, he said, "Okay. After the round sometime."

After Eddie had walked off, shoulders back, chin up, as if daring anyone to challenge him, Pat rejoined Carol. Handing her a mug of black coffee, she said, "Have you watched his sister play? She's going to be a sensation on the American circuit because—"

Pat broke off as an announcement that play in the Whitlew Challenge was resuming boomed through the public address system. Immediately a general exodus began, and soon Carol and Pat were almost the only people left in the lounge.

Carol, being far more interested at the moment in what Pat knew about Gussie than Brinella Altunga's chances on the LPGA circuit, said, "How well do you know Gussie Whitlew?"

"She's very active in the art world. You can rely on Gussie to be at every function that high society supports, but she also attends openings at little galleries. She's genuinely interested in art, which is all too rare in her group."

"Her group being?"

"The megarich. I first met Gussie years ago, when her husband was alive, and I've been running into her at art shows ever since. When she likes someone's work, she buys up big, so any gallery owner exhibiting new talent prays to have an exhibition where Gussie is bowled over by the artist's work."

"Has your gallery been lucky?" Carol asked.

"Were we ever!" Pat exulted. "Heard of Eidleen Trotter? She's a sculptor who does some really bizarre stuff. Gussie fell in love with one particular piece, but another well-known art collector, Wilson Graham, wanted it too and was prepared to pay a premium for it."

"Who won?"

Pat shook her head. "Carol, I can tell you that I'd never get in that woman's way if she wanted something."

"She had Wilson Graham killed?" said Carol, joking.

"She didn't need to, although I wouldn't have put it past her, if all else failed. Actually, what Gussie did was tell Eidleen that if the sculpture was sold to Graham, Gussie would use every bit of influence she had to make sure Eidleen got nowhere in the Sydney art market. If Gussie got the item, she'd boost Eidleen's career."

"I can guess what happened."

"Gussie got the sculpture, titled, by the way, *Woman on the Edge of Something Big*, and Eidleen's career got the promised boost." Pat grinned at Carol. "Don't cross Gussie Whitlew—the woman's dangerous."

* * *

Beth Shima was on her way out to the course when Carol stopped her. After introducing herself, Carol said, "Ms. Shima, I've just got one quick question. What did Fiona Hawk talk to you about at the reception on Thursday night?"

Beth had inky black hair and almond eyes, but none of the fabled inscrutability of the East. She giggled, then said in a distinct American accent, "Like always, Fiona was trying to psych me out. There were five ahead of me on the leader board, but she knew that I'm a slow starter and usually get going on the second day."

"That's all?"

Suddenly serious, Beth Shima said, "Well, no." She wriggled her shoulders. "I suppose it doesn't matter now, but I promised Fiona not to tell anyone. She was upset about a guy, said he'd been screwing her around. Said she'd had enough. Fiona knew I'd just broken up with my boyfriend, so I guess she thought I'd understand."

"Did she mention the name of this guy?"

"Sure," said Beth. "Liam Ivanovich. I don't know who she caught him with, but she was really shocked, and that surprised me. Fiona, I thought, was shockproof."

* * *

Ralph Syncomm was drowning his sorrows in one of the two clubhouse bars when Carol found him. He took a long swallow of beer, then snapped, "What do you want?"

"Before you give a formal statement to Sergeant Bourke, I'd like an informal discussion."

Suspicious, he glared at her. "What about?"

"What sort of relationship did Fiona have with Liam Ivanovich?"

He smirked. "Sex, sex, and more sex."

"Anything more?"

He threw back his head and drained his glass, then gestured to the barman for another drink. "Fiona was very possessive. On top of that, although she acted cool in public, I happen to know for a fact she was totally obsessed with him."

"How did you know this? Did she confide in you?"

He sniggered. "Fiona? Confide? No way. Ivanovich told me." He broke off to signal impatiently. "Hey, you, behind the bar. Another beer."

"Mr. Ivanovich told you details about this relationship?"

"Yeah, he let drop a few things. He's the jealous sort. Liked to control her. In private, he treated Fiona badly, but she just kept on going back for more." Syncomm smiled sourly. "Fought like cat and dog. Always made up, though, until this last time. I don't know who she caught him with, but Fiona blew her top. Told Ivanovich she was through with him, both professionally and privately."

"You didn't think to mention this before?"

Syncomm assumed a virtuous air. "Personal matter, isn't it?" he said. "Fiona wouldn't have wanted me talking about it."

* * *

Mark Bourke was laughing when she found him with Anne Newsome in Gussie's office. "I was just telling Anne about your dear aunt's travails," he said.

"Aunt Sarah's been arrested?"

"She's mad as a hornet, but not because she's been arrested—she didn't persuade the cops to do that. No, it's the parking ticket they issued her that's got her really upset."

"Did the protest get any TV coverage?"

"That's the silver lining," said Bourke. "Aunt Sarah says she's been assured that her Eco-Crones will be featured on at least two newscasts tonight. It didn't totally assuage the pain of the parking ticket, but it helped."

Carol eyed a carafe of coffee sitting on a tray with cups and what looked like cucumber sandwiches cut into neat triangles. "Is that coffee hot?"

"Fresh from the kitchen." As Bourke poured her a cup, he said, "Coop picked up one of the boys—Ken Lawson. Terry sat in on the interview, and he says the kid absolutely denies being on the golf course on Thursday night. Terry says Coop's sure he's lying, but he's sticking to his story."

"What about the other boy?"

"Justin Mott? He's missing. Lives with his mother, and she isn't the slightest worried. Says he goes off with friends for days at a time and he'll turn up when he feels like it."

Carol took a sip of her coffee, making a mental note to think seriously about cutting down on the amount of caffeine she ingested. One day, when she wasn't in the middle of an investigation...

"It's just too coincidental, this kid's missing. Can we get a photo from his mother?"

"Already done," said Bourke. "It's going to media outlets as we speak. And I've sent Terry back to headquarters—there's plenty for him to do there." Amused, he added, "Terry wasn't a bit pleased. He practically begged me to let him stay. Oh, and before I forget, he did leave a message for you: No bodies floated in on the tide along this part of the coast."

Anne Newsome reported on her calls to Ireland. She'd spoken to one of Ivanovich's sisters and also to the local police. His mother had died, and there was a family business—but her death had been two weeks ago, and there had been no talk of Liam coming home for the funeral or to help with the business. "He wasn't close to his mother," said Anne. "In fact, reading between the lines, it seems he didn't much care for her at all."

Bourke had interviewed Mick Slane, who had been the replacement caddie for Fiona Hawk on Thursday. It had all been strictly business. She hadn't been friendly, didn't ask his advice about choice of clubs, and had conferred with him only about a couple of the more difficult holes.

Hefting a stack of printouts, Anne said, "Disappointing news. No ax murderers or serial killers on the Whitlew staff. Some unpaid traffic tickets, one failure to pay child support, and two drunk and disorderly arrests. That's it."

Carol told them about Beth Shima's conversation with Fiona and about Ralph Syncomm's version of the relationship between Fiona and her caddie.

"It'll be interesting to hear Ivanovich's side of the story," said Bourke. "I'll grab him when he comes off the course."

* * *

Carol saw Anne blink when Liam Ivanovich came into the office with Bourke. This was not the first time Anne had seen him, as she'd taken notes at the first interview, but Carol had to agree that the effect the man had was not blunted by familiarity.

She decided it wasn't just that Liam Ivanovich was extraordinarily handsome, nor was it the contrast between his white skin, black hair, and deep blue eyes. He had a disturbing sexual presence, as though he was only just holding himself in check.

Carol said, "Thank you for making time for us, Mr. Ivanovich."

"I had a choice?"

Carol smiled slightly. "Your mother died two weeks ago."

He looked at her warily. "And your point...?"

"My point is that you implied that her death had just occurred."

"You misunderstood me."

"You said in the earlier interview that you told Fiona Hawk that you had to return to Ireland because your mother had suddenly passed away. But that wasn't true, was it?"

"So she died a few days earlier. What's the problem?"

"You also said that you had a sexual relationship with Ms. Hawk, but there were, as you put it, no strings attached. Is that right?"

"That's right."

"We've heard other opinions regarding the closeness of your relationship, and they describe it rather differently. Ms. Hawk is depicted as being obsessed with you, and you are described as jealous and controlling."

He settled back in the chair, crossing his arms across his chest. "People can think what they like."

"Fiona Hawk fired you on that Wednesday because, as she told a witness, you were screwing around."

He straightened, shoving out his chin belligerently. "Who told you that?"

"Fiona surprised you with someone. Who was it?"

Ivanovich pressed his lips together, his face impassive.

"Mr. Ivanovich?"

"I don't kiss and tell."

Bourke, who'd been sitting quietly to one side, said, "Where were you Thursday evening?"

Ivanovich leapt to his feet. "You're not going to pin Fiona's murder on me!"

Bourke didn't seem to move rapidly, but before Ivanovich could take a step, Bourke was in front of him. "Sit down, Mr. Ivanovich. The Inspector hasn't finished." Bourke put a hand on Ivanovich's chest and, without seeming to exert much force, slammed him back into his seat.

"Now," said Carol, "where were you on Thursday evening?"

CHAPTER FIFTEEN

It was almost midnight when Carol reached Leota's hotel. After taking Ivanovich's formal statement—he continued to deny that Fiona had fired him, and claimed to have spent the Thursday night she died on a solitary pub crawl that got him back to his hotel at one in the morning—Carol had interviewed Brinella, with Eddie insisting he be present. Brinella had confirmed that what Eddie had told Carol was accurate.

Gussie, when Carol found her later, at first had been angry, then embarrassed about Brinella seeing her in the equipment room on Thursday. "If you must know," she said, "I was leaving a gift of jewelry in Fiona's golf bag. I fully expected her to spend Thursday night with me, and this little present, which she'd find the next day, was going to show...well, my appreciation." She had reddened even further as she added, "On Friday, when I found out what had happened to Fiona, I retrieved the gift. I'd written a rather graphic card to go with it."

Then Carol had spent hours going through statements with Bourke and looking at the as yet incomplete telephone records for the mobile phones Gussie had distributed so generously to her players. She'd called Aunt Sarah at Sybil's, commiserated with her nonarrest, and told her that it was no use asking— there was no way Carol could cancel the parking ticket.

Now, so close to Leota, the certainty Carol had been feeling all day dissolved into doubt. Why was she betting so much on a relationship with someone who was in many ways a stranger?

The hotel corridor was hushed, filled only with the faint whisper of air conditioning, so that when she rapped on Leota's door the noise seemed sharp and intrusive. She had raised her hand to knock again, when the door opened.

"My very own detective inspector."

Carol was swept into a hard embrace. "Perhaps I could get inside first?" she protested.

"Perhaps you could." Leota released her and shut the door with care, so that the lock clicked into place softly.

They hadn't seen each other for months but had spoken often, developing the special intimacy that came from listening for the nuances and shades in another person's voice. Abruptly, Carol's reservations seemed ridiculous. Leota was as Carol remembered her—sure and strong.

"You don't seem jetlagged," Carol remarked. "Isn't your body clock telling you it's five o'clock in the morning?"

Leota laughed, her teeth white in her dark face. "My body clock is telling me, quite insistently, that it's time for you."

She put her head to one side and looked Carol over. "You've lost weight, darling, and you can't afford to. I'd like to think it was fretting for me, but I imagine it's your work. You've had a hard time, these past months, haven't you?"

To her absolute amazement, Carol felt tears prick her eyes. Leota must have seen something in her face, because she stepped forward and, gentle now, took Carol in her arms.

Carol said against her neck, "I'm tired, and emotional." She chuckled. "Actually, that's the code our media use when they want to say that some public figure is falling-down drunk."

"Are you angling for champagne?"

"No. You're intoxicating enough."

"Ah," said Leota, "I love romantic talk."

"Shall we kiss?" said Carol. "It's customary."

She remembered, with sudden, total recall, the first time they had kissed. It had been slow, sweet, with no urgency. That was not the way she felt tonight.

"The last time we made love," said Leota, "you were bruised and battered and had, if I recollect, two cracked ribs."

"All healed."

"Is your heart healed too?"

Carol frowned at her. "My heart? What do you mean?"

Leota looked disconcerted, as though she hadn't meant to ask the question. "I'm not sure what I mean. Forget I said it." She put up a hand to cup the side of Carol's face. "But remember I adore you."

They kissed, not gently at all. A jolt of passion transfixed Carol. Her pulse throbbed, her control shattered. "Fast," she said, "and hard."

"Not my style."

"Make it your style."

Leota laughed, a low, arousing sound. "Yes, ma'am!"

The anonymous hotel room faded away. The world became bare skin and beating hearts. They contended together, two warriors fighting for the same prize.

Simmering heat burst into raw craving. Carol writhed with it, cried out for satiation—for pure sensation to dissolve her thoughts, her heart, the self at her core. To make her body thrash with longing, to transmute her into something new—a singing, golden note, struck hard and ringing.

"I love you," she heard Leota say, just as the center of her flamed, rippled, then tossed her back into the tangled sheets of a hotel bed.

A delicious, honeyed lassitude flowed through Carol. She was too gorgeously fatigued to move.

"How was it?" Leota was smug.

Trying to slow her breathing, Carol said, "Okay, I guess."

Mock outrage. "Just okay!"

"Oh, all right. Sensational. Incendiary."

"That's more like it."

* * *

Carol swam up to the surface of consciousness, reluctant to let go the dream that held her. Somewhere, an insistent sound was repeating. She opened her eyes to Leota's sleeping face, smiled, then sighed. Her mobile phone was calling her, as insistent as an alarm.

She half fell out of the bed, fumbled with her discarded clothes, and found it shrieking in her jacket pocket. "Yes?"

"Carol—sorry to disturb you. When I didn't get you at home, I tried your mobile."

"What is it?"

"Justin Mott. He's dead. His body was found washed up on the little beach near the country club."

"I'm on my way."

CHAPTER SIXTEEN

Driving through the gray, predawn light, Carol struggled to put the joys of the night behind her and concentrate on the corpse that was waiting for her. Even if Justin Mott had been a vandal, a bully who preyed on homeless people, he was still a young man at the beginning of his years. Who was to say that he might not have turned himself around and led a good and happy life? Now all those possibilities had been snuffed out.

She turned onto a road that ran straight to the water. The country club was half a kilometer to the north. Ahead she could see a clump of cars, parked haphazardly as law enforcement vehicles often were.

Carol had to clamber down a short but steep path to the tiny beach. There was a strong smell of seaweed, and she could hear the alternating suck and whoosh of the waves as they flirted with the beach. The fiery rim of the sun was just showing as she reached the group standing on the sand. "It's Justin Mott," said Bourke. "He's got a fake ID to get him into pubs in that name, and the photo seems to match."

They stood back to let Carol view the body. Justin was puffy from immersion, his face swollen and heavy. His skull was deformed and had clearly been crushed by some great force.

"I reckon he fell on his head from a great height," said Bourke. "Dived off a cliff or fell when climbing. Or maybe someone pushed him."

"Someone pushed him," said Carol.

* * *

Bourke took Carol to the nearest McDonald's for breakfast. He ate heartily; she examined hers with doubt, and concentrated on her coffee instead.

"So," said Bourke through a mouthful, "Justin Mott sees far too much on the fourth hole on Thursday night. On Friday he tries to collect on what he's seen. He finds his target uncooperative, and one way or another, he sustains massive head injuries, probably from a dive onto rocks, where his body is picked up by the tide and floated out to sea."

"Establishing time of death is going to be a killer," said Carol, adding, "Pun intended," when Bourke groaned.

Carol finally took a bite of her breakfast and found it much better than she had expected. Suddenly, she was hungry.

"Mark, what would shock someone like Fiona Hawk? Whatever it was that made her break up with Ivanovich, it was a real jolt to her."

"Finding he preferred someone else to her would be a shock," said Bourke with a cynical smile.

"Beth Shima said that Fiona was shockproof, but this time was different." Carol checked out the menu above the counter, trying to decide if she wanted something else to eat. A sudden thought brought her attention back to Bourke. "Fiona hated homosexuality."

They looked at each other. "He was with a man," said Bourke. "Fiona caught Ivanovich with another man."

"Gussie said Davy Vere was bisexual," said Carol. "Let's have a chat with him."

* * *

As it was the last day of the tournament, Gussie and her staff were at the country club early. Carol and Bourke found Davy Vere in one of the offices with Gussie, running through items for the final ceremony, where the first and second place-getters would receive their trophies and, more important, their prize money.

Vere had on tight tan leather pants and a black leather vest. He glowered at them when they appeared. He said, "I'm too busy," when Carol requested his presence. "Ask Gussie. She'll tell you I can't be spared."

With a wicked smile, Gussie said, "You can have him if you let me call you Carol."

"The missing boy who was on the course on Thursday night has been found," said Carol. "He's dead. It is very likely a second murder, so I'd appreciate Mr. Vere's immediate cooperation."

"Oh my God," said Gussie. "Go on, Davy—I can look after things here."

Vere led the way to Gussie's office, impatiently striding ahead of them. He sat down, frowning, and said to Carol, "I have nothing to do with killing this kid. I don't even know his name."

"I'd like to take you back to Thursday. When you spoke with Fiona Hawk, you weren't discussing the possibility of sex with her, you were discussing something else altogether."

"Yeah? Then why did Ruth Gallant say I'd put the hard word on Fiona if it wasn't true?"

Carol said, "You tried to emphasize that the conflict with Fiona was about you propositioning her by pressuring Ruth Gallant to change her story, which made me pay more attention to it."

Smothering a yawn, Vere said, "Sounds farfetched to me."

Bourke said, "Fiona caught you and Liam Ivanovich in what I'll call a compromising position."

"Jesus," said Davy Vere, "can't you call a spade a spade?" He shook his head testily. "All right, I'll tell you. Fiona walked into Liam's hotel room to find us hard at it. It was almost funny, the way she carried on. She sobbed—you know, I think she really cared for him, poor bitch. And then she lost it, started screaming insults, and ended up firing him."

Carol thought that Vere seemed almost relieved to be telling the story, so she prompted him to continue by saying, "And then what did Mr. Ivanovich do?"

"Liam tried to talk her round. Being her caddie paid very well and had lots of perks. And, as Fiona had an excellent chance of winning this tournament, he didn't want to kiss good-bye to his bonus of one-fifty thousand."

"Did she calm down?"

"No, but Liam tried again later, after I'd gone. He promised Fiona what she'd seen meant nothing, but she didn't want to believe that. She offered to pay his airfare back to Ireland, just to get rid of him. Liam said he'd go, but he didn't mean to. He told me he'd let her cool down for a day, struggle along with some other caddie, and then he'd turn up and give her the 'I love you and I can't leave you' story."

"Do you believe that's what he intended to do?" Carol inquired.

Davy Vere sat forward, his eyes boring into Carol's. "Look, if you think Liam murdered Fiona, then think again. Why would he kill the golden goose?"

"Does Ms. Whitlew know all about this?"

Vere gave a snort of laughter. "Tell Gussie? No way! More than my job's worth—she'd be absolutely furious if she thought I had anything to do with upsetting one of her precious golfers. I told her Fiona and Liam parted good friends, just to cover myself."

* * *

Coop, flint faced, said, "Well, Inspector, I've got the other boy for you—Ken Lawson." He looked past Carol to Mark

Bourke and jerked his head in acknowledgment. "Bourke," he said with no suggestion of welcome.

He led the way to the interview room, saying, "I'll sit in, okay?" Carol nodded. Coop went on, "Ken Lawson's dad's here too. *Very* outraged that we cops might think his bloody kid's involved in any way. He's refusing to let the little tick give a statement."

Mr. Lawson got to his feet the moment the door opened. He was short, red faced, and anxious. Carol had seen parents like him before. He was frightened at what his son might have done, and was covering the fear with belligerence.

"Why are we being held here?" he demanded. "Ken hasn't committed any crime. I'll be getting a lawyer if you keep this up. Wrongful arrest, that's what it is."

Carol sighed to herself, knowing all too well Mr. Lawson's type. Whatever his personal misgivings about his offspring, he would continue to insist his son could do no wrong, no matter how convincing the evidence to the contrary.

She introduced herself and Bourke, then said, "We're investigating two murders. Ken appears to be a material witness to at least one of them. That is why we require a full statement from him regarding his activities over the past few days."

"Activities? It's that Mott boy you should be blaming, not Ken. Ken's done nothing wrong, and you can't keep us here." He motioned furiously to the weedy, pimply boy sitting with straight-backed tension on one of the uncomfortable wooden chairs. "Come on, Ken."

"Mr. Lawson," said Carol, "your son is not under arrest at this time, but if you attempt to remove him from this room, I *will* arrest him for trespassing on the Whitlew Country Club grounds. That charge will certainly hold him under lock and key at least until a magistrate's court on Monday."

Lawson glared at her. Carol gazed calmly back. Coop, over in a corner, smirked. After a few moments Lawson dropped his glance. "What are you asking?"

"I'm asking for Ken to truthfully tell us everything he knows. You will be present throughout the entire interview, which will be taped. After Ken's statement is typed up, Ken will read it, sign it, and you can both go home."

Lawson sat down heavily in the nearest chair. "All right, go ahead, but I want it on record that I don't like it."

Mark Bourke conducted most of the interview, with a question now and then from Carol. Ken Lawson, one of the most unprepossessing youths that Carol had ever set eyes upon, scratched at his scalp, picked at the blemishes on his face, sniffed incessantly—he obviously had a sinus problem—and generally made an unpleasant impression.

"It's all Justin's fault," he whined before Bourke had asked his first question. "He was the one that got me in trouble. I didn't do nothing."

With reluctance Ken admitted that he and Justin, sometimes with other friends, had frequently roughed up the occupants of the camp in the nature reserve, although he described it as "having a bit of fun."

When had he last seen Justin? Ken wriggled around on his chair, finally admitting to Bourke that it had been Thursday night, around nine-thirty or ten, on the golf course.

"What were you doing there?" interposed Carol. Ken looked at his father, then at Carol. "Just fooling around."

"What sort of fooling around?" Carol's voice had an edge to it. "This is a double murder case. We're not interested in charging you with anything petty, such as trespass, unless you fail to cooperate."

"I'd take that as a threat!" exclaimed Mr. Lawson, half rising from his chair.

"It is, in fact, a promise to prosecute your son to the full extent of the law if he neglects to tell the whole truth," said Carol. Lawson sank back.

His son said, "We were going to...you know...muck up the place a bit."

"Intention to commit vandalism," said Bourke, his voice stern. "Now that's much more serious than simple trespass."

"We never did nothing," protested Ken. "Like, we never got a chance, see? We heard this fight—a couple of people yelling at each other—and Justin said we should go and have a dekko, okay? See what was going on."

Carol's hopes that she might have an actual witness to Fiona Hawk's murder faded as it became apparent that, along with his other shortcomings, Ken lacked daring. "It was real creepy out there, know what I mean? Like it was all black in the shadows, and suddenly all the yelling stopped, and I said I didn't want to get too close, but Justin went on."

"And you?" said Bourke.

"I got the hell out of there." He looked rather pleased with himself as he added, "Looks like I did the right thing, don't it, when you see what happened to Justin."

"What did happen to Justin?" asked Carol.

Ken licked his lips. "Well, he got killed." He leaned forward, confidentially, apparently more at ease now he had told most of his story. "I didn't see him after Thursday, but I rang him on Friday, just to find out what went on, and Justin said he was going to make quite a bit of money. Said to come and get pissed with him Friday night, to celebrate."

Ken forestalled the next question with a resentful explanation. "My mum wouldn't let me go. She grounded me."

"You see?" said Mr. Lawson. "Ken has nothing to do with whatever happened to Mott."

"There was no suggestion that he was involved," said Carol.

Ken was drooping over the table, rather teary eyed. "Jeez," he said, "Justin was happy, that last telephone call. He was laughing so hard…"

That seemed to be the total of what Ken knew, as further questions gained nothing more. He was vague about the voices—thought one was a female but couldn't be sure of the other. After Justin had gone on to investigate, Ken had got out of the country club grounds as fast as he could.

"How about security on the course?" Carol asked.

Ken snickered. "Oh yeah, right. Like, there wasn't any, see? Anyone could get in—or out."

His statement was typed, read, signed, and Mr. Lawson and his obnoxious son dispatched homeward.

Coop, rocking on his heels, hands in pockets, observed, "Blackmail, pure and simple. The Mott kid saw enough to be dangerous to someone. He was dumb enough to try the extort some money, and got himself killed for his pains."

Carol didn't find herself agreeing with Coop often, but this time she couldn't fault his succinct summation. It was almost certainly true that Justin Mott had brought his violent death upon himself.

* * *

They heard Charlene Mott before they saw her. "Yeah, yeah, hang on, will ya!"

She opened the door and glowered at them. "What-cha want? If you're reporters, you can go fuck yourselves, right? I got a contract, see, and I can only speak to that bunch."

She had stringy blond hair, showing dark at the roots. Barefoot, she held a grubby floral housecoat shut with one hand. In her other hand she had a cigarette, burnt almost down to her fingers. She sucked a jolt of nicotine from it, then flicked the lighted butt out into the wasteland that in neighboring houses was the front garden, but here was sour, neglected dirt.

When Carol introduced herself and Bourke, Charlene Mott's scowl deepened. "Ah, Jesus, more cops. Just what I need. Look, I identified Justin, smashed up like he was. And I said I didn't know where he'd been, okay? I got nothing more to say."

"We have a few further questions," said Carol. "If you don't wish to answer them here, we'd be pleased to take you down to the station if that's more convenient."

The woman shoved her face close to Carol's. "Yeah, right. Go on and threaten me. And me with my boy dead. I told Detective Bloody Coop that I knew my rights, and I'll tell you that too."

Carol didn't step back, although Charlene Mott's breath was an offensive weapon in its own right. "Ms. Mott—it will be here, or at the station," Carol said. "Your choice."

"Oh, all right. Come in."

The hallway was dingy, the walls smeared with grime. The fusty odor of neglect filled the air. The living room was hardly an improvement. A big-screen television blared in one corner, the only modern item. The sofa and two matching chairs were covered with torn, stained, yellow vinyl. The design of the carpet was almost impossible to discern under the layers of dirt. A coffee table was covered with magazines, dirty plates, glasses, an overflowing ashtray, a soup dish filled with salted peanuts, several cans of Foster's beer, and the remains of a pizza in an open cardboard box, around which several flies circled and dived.

"Make yourself at home," said Charlene Mott with a feral grin. She slumped into one of the yellow chairs and grabbed the remote, extinguishing the television. There was a carton of cigarettes on the floor near her bare feet. She picked it up, ripped it open, and extracted a pack. Fixing Carol with narrowed eyes, she said combatively, "And don't tell me I can't smoke in me own house."

Carol and Bourke, after exchanging a mutually appalled glance, had selected to sit on the least filthy area of the yellow sofa, although neither was willing to lean back into its dusty embrace.

Carol said a few polite words of condolence, earning an impatient, "Yeah, yeah."

Bourke said, "You weren't concerned when your son didn't return home on Friday night?"

The bereaved mother took a hard drag on her freshly lit cigarette, then blew a blue cloud of smoke in their direction. "Justin had done it plenty of times before—stayed out overnight. Since he was little, he's been the bane of my bloody life, I can tell you. So I didn't think anything of it. Long time since I've given a shit where the little bugger might be."

She took a handful of peanuts and crammed them into her mouth, chewed, then washed everything down with a long swallow from her can of Foster's.

Carol said, "Justin has a friend named Ken. Do you know him?"

"Sure I do. Why aren't you after him, then? Him and his bloody father. Ken'd know more than me about what Justin was up to."

"When did you last see your son?"

"I dunno. Friday afternoon, around five or sixish." She scratched the back of her neck and sighed, not, Carol thought, with any vestige of sorrow, but rather with irritation. "I asked him where he was going, and he said, 'Out.' He always said that."

Carol said, "Did you notice anything unusual about Justin's manner, or anything he said?"

Charlene Mott tilted her head back, apparently looking for inspiration from the peeling ceiling. "You know," she said, "there was something. Justin was real pleased with himself, like he was going to get laid, you know? Kept smiling to himself. Asked him what the big secret was, and he told me to mind my own business."

"Had he received any messages? Phone calls?"

"Yeah, there were some calls, but there always were, so nothing out of the ordinary with that."

"And on Friday?"

"Yeah, now I think of it, the telephone did ring right before he went out." Putting out her cigarette with vicious stabs, she added, "And don't ask me who it was. I never answered the phone when he was home. He got nasty if I did."

They could get nothing more from her, so with the admonition that there might be further questions in the future, Carol and Bourke escaped to the delight of the clean outside air.

"Mother love," said Bourke. "You can't beat it."

CHAPTER SEVENTEEN

The monitor in Gussie's office was showing the final day's play of the Whitlew Challenge. The sound was muted, but every now and then Carol glanced up to catch the leader board. On Saturday the top three had been Ashleigh Piddock, Toni Karstares, and Brinella Altunga, and then a gap to Beth Shima and Susann Johansson. Kasha London, who'd fallen back in the field on Friday, had considerably improved her position by the end of play on Saturday, coming back after the rain interruption to pick up several shots, while some of the players who had been in front of her struggled to cope with the wet course.

Today the lead kept changing, with Toni Karstares and Susann Johansson dueling for the top spot and Brinella Altunga just two shots back. Kasha was making a late run and had improved to be within four of the lead.

The golf course looked beautiful on the screen, and Carol longed to be outside. Sunday, which had begun for Carol with Justin Mott's sodden body on the beach, had developed into one of those late summer days she loved—not too hot, but full of golden warmth. She'd lingered outside to watch the early players, who had little hope of finishing in any substantial money, tee off.

Now, inside with the beauties of the day secondhand through the monitor screen, Carol was restless. Tomorrow most of the players she was watching would leave Australia, and she chafed at the thought that a murderer might be escaping her.

"We need to know who called Charlene Mott's number on Friday night. It has to be the murderer, setting up a meeting," said Carol.

Bourke looked at Anne, who was sitting in the corner of Gussie's office, peering into a laptop screen. "Yet another phone for you to check, Anne."

"Oh good. I was getting bored." She made a face. "Do you have any idea how many calls these golfing women make? Curse Gussie Whitlew for providing them with mobile phones."

"Print everything out—Mark and I will go through them too. And, Mark, I want photos and postmortem diagrams of Fiona Hawk's head injury, and forensics' description of the blood on the head of the club, and—" She stopped.

"What's up?" said Bourke.

"Grab that magnifying glass, Mark. Have you looked at these photos Hilary O'Dell took at the Thursday night reception?"

"Not yet. Am I looking for something specific?"

"It's a long shot, but yes—a bracelet."

* * *

Bourke said, "I wouldn't like to go to court with what we've got. We haven't got any evidence that any half-good legal eagle can't explain away. For example, the call to Justin Mott on Friday was made from a phone in the country club's offices, and it could be anyone."

"The log at the front gate shows she lied about leaving her car here on Friday night. She arranged to pick Justin Mott up, and took him somewhere close to murder him."

"You know that isn't enough. There're ways to explain it away."

"Then," said Carol, "what we need is a full confession."

Bourke looked at her with a raised eyebrow. "Carol, exactly how do you propose to achieve that?"

"I'll get wired, have a chat with our murderer, and record our conversation."

"You make it sound so simple…"

* * *

Gussie, looking quite splendid in a white silk pantsuit, presided over the awarding of the trophies. A large crowd had gathered around the tables bearing the extremely ugly crystal trophies—the largest for the winner, the lesser one for second place.

"And in the inaugural Whitlew Challenge Cup, it is my great pleasure to award the first trophy in this prestigious new tournament to Toni Karstares. Thank you, Toni, for a consummate display of golfing skill."

Toni Karstares made a short speech, speaking glowingly of the Whitlew Challenge, and Carol, watching, smiled to see Gussie exult in the praise.

Susann Johansson was the runner-up, and made a gracious tribute in a charming accent, commending Gussie Whitlew for her generous gifts to the women's golfing world.

There was no official presentation for third place, but Kasha London had taken this position, and a substantial monetary reward.

The ceremonies over, the crowd began to disperse. Carol said, "Walk with me, it's a beautiful day."

Kasha London hesitated, then said, "Okay."

"Congratulations on your win. You made a wonderful run at the end, and I thought you might even catch the leader."

Glowing with pleasure, Kasha said, "Thank you. I did play well."

After a few moments she asked, "How are your investigations going?"

"Very well."

Kasha seemed surprised. "You're near an arrest?"

Carol nodded. "We have a suspect, and we're just checking on a few outstanding details."

"Can I ask who it is?"

"Liam Ivanovich."

Kasha abruptly halted. She could hardly have looked more astonished. "*Liam?* You must be joking."

"You know him well. Don't you think he's capable of murder?"

"I suppose anyone's capable given the right circumstances, but Liam didn't kill Fiona."

They began to stroll again, Carol leading the way onto the course. "He's an attractive man," she said. "Are you close?"

Kasha went to answer, paused, then said, "Yes, actually we *are* close." She paused again, then said with a rush of pride, "Actually, we're in love."

"I see."

Her face suddenly suffused with red, Kasha said, "I shouldn't have said that. I suppose you think it's hilarious, me being in love with Liam Ivanovich."

"Of course not, but I thought he was sleeping with Fiona Hawk."

"Oh, that was almost over. She was a prima donna. Liam was tired of her, but he wanted to get the Whitlew Challenge over before he broke it off."

They were approaching the cliffs, and Carol paused to admire the view. "Beautiful, isn't it?"

"Beautiful," said Kasha absently, looking not at the scenery, but at Carol. "How can you think Liam killed Fiona?"

"Didn't she find out that he was having a relationship with Davy Vere?"

"She freaked, but Liam told me it was just a walk on the wild side—just an experiment."

"So it didn't worry you?"

"I didn't care, just so long as it wasn't another woman."

"That other woman—Fiona," said Carol. "How did you get her up onto this headland?"

"I don't know what you mean."

Carol smiled, an understanding, sympathetic smile. "We both know what I mean."

She saw Kasha look around, see that they were quite alone, and make a decision. Kasha said, "Fiona said to me that Liam turned her on, like nobody else had ever done. She thought he'd left the country, and now that she'd cooled off, she was really upset about it. When I told her at the reception he was still in Australia, she didn't believe me, so I gave her the number of his new hotel and told her to check."

"What if he'd answered the phone?"

"I knew he wasn't there. He's an Irishman—he'd gone out drinking." Her indulgent smiled faded as she went on with distaste, "Fiona was so thrilled, she nearly cried. Made me sick to see her. I said that Liam had sent me to talk with her, and see if she would forgive him, because he wanted to make up."

"He knew nothing about this?"

"Of course not. He would have only got in the way. When I told Fiona that Liam was at the country club and had gone for a walk up to the fourth hole, hoping against hope that she would join him, she couldn't wait. I left with her, said I'd show her exactly where he was. She didn't want me there, but was so keen to see him, it hardly mattered to her."

"Justin Mott heard an argument."

Kasha made a scornful sound. "Motherfucker."

"What went wrong with Fiona?"

"It was easy going, because of the moonlight. Everything was fine, and Fiona was going on about how she loved Liam and he loved her. I couldn't stand it, so I told her we were lovers." Kasha smiled at the thought. "Fiona was so angry. Told me how he could never love some over-the-hill bitch like me. I was pleased she said that, because it made it all the easier to kill her."

"You had planned ahead."

"I had. Used a master key from administration and took Brinella's sand wedge, and just as it was getting dark I took a walk up here and hid it in the bushes near the bunker."

"Why get Brinella involved?"

"She's just like Fiona. Everything goes right for her. Brinella's the wonder black girl, isn't she? Toast of Australia. Took the circuit LPGA by storm. It was about time there was a wrinkle in her fairy story."

Knowing that with a murder like this, anticipation was half the reward for the murderer, Carol said, "You planned it well. It must have pleased you that everything went so smoothly. Did Fiona realize what was happening at the end?"

"I hope so. I took the club from the bushes. It shone bright in the moonlight, and Fiona said, 'What are you doing?' and I said, 'Killing you,' and I hit her. She went down, and I pulled her into the bunker, laid her out neatly and, when I'd got myself positioned for a good shot, I swung the club at her head. It made the oddest sound—a sort of wet, crackling thud." She let out a long sigh. "She never would have let Liam go."

"You made a mistake—your bracelet."

"But don't you admire how I covered for it? I must have broken the catch dragging Fiona onto the bunker, and raked over it when I was smoothing the sand. When I realized I'd lost it somewhere, I made up my locker story so that you'd think someone was deliberately trying to incriminate me. It worked, didn't it?"

"Oh yes, it worked," said Carol with a deliberate touch of admiration. Kasha smiled. Carol said, "And Justin Mott?"

"He stopped me, just when I got to my car, said he'd seen what I'd done and he wanted money. I knew then I had to kill him. I played along, took his telephone number, and said I'd get whatever he wanted."

"How much was he asking?"

"Only five thousand, but that was the first demand. Others would follow. He thought he could blackmail me, the stupid little fuck, and because he was a male, and bigger and taller than me, he thought he was safe. Stupid, vicious creep."

"You met him on Friday night?"

"I told Gussie I had a migraine, so I didn't have to waste time talking to you. Called him, picked him up and took him down the end of the road near the club. 'Show me,' I said, 'I won't pay until I'm sure you saw something.' He was so stupid that he followed me up to the fourth hole, thinking he was safe. I had a small wrench from the car with me, hidden. He was overconfident. He went over near the edge, I hit him, he went over. Never even screamed."

"Efficient," said Carol, "but you've made two mistakes."

"What mistakes?"

"There's a photograph of you taken on Thursday night, and you're wearing the bracelet. I don't imagine you went back to your locker after the reception, so how could you leave it there to be stolen?"

"What else?"

"You're left handed. The forensic evidence is that a wedge angled for a right-handed player, was used by someone left-handed."

Unimpressed, Kasha said, "If I hadn't explained everything, you'd never have known for sure. You think you're going to arrest me now, don't you?" She jerked her head in the direction of the cliff. "Or perhaps you think I'll break down and say I can't go on and conveniently throw myself onto the rocks down there."

"What I think is, we're going to walk back to the country club together."

Kasha gave her a long look. "All right."

The attack came when Carol expected it—almost immediately. Carol sidestepped Kasha's rush, seized her arm, and braced the elbow until Kasha fell to her knees in pain.

"Kasha London, I arrest you for the murder of Fiona Hawk. I must warn you that anything—"

Kasha screamed, a primal, gut-rending sound. It rang out over the green slopes, and echoed in Carol's mind like a banshee predicting death. It took a moment for her to realize the word she was shrieking. It was Liam's name.

* * *

"Kasha?" Gussie's voice rose to a screech. "First Fiona, and now Kasha London? The Whitlew Challenge will have the reputation of a death tournament! I'll be the Typhoid Mary of the golfing world!"

CHAPTER EIGHTEEN

"What are you thinking?" Carol asked. She was sitting with Leota on the back deck of her house. Aunt Sarah was inside, cooking her latest specialty, vegetarian lasagna.

"I'm thinking of our golden future."

"That's nice," said Carol, "but there are difficulties, little things like the fact we live on different continents and have demanding jobs that can't be moved."

"Not altogether true," said Leota. "I'm not promising anything, but there's a possibility I can arrange a transfer to Australia in an FBI liaison position. If it comes off, it might not be ideal, because I probably won't be in Sydney all the time, but at least I'd be on the same continent."

"I can cope with that," said Carol, seeing horizons expanding as she watched.

Bella Books, Inc.

Women. Books. Even Better Together.

P.O. Box 10543
Tallahassee, FL 32302

Phone: 800-729-4992
www.bellabooks.com